This is meant to be the real me, this is meant to be the whole truth. And now that truth might be awkward or embarrassing, or difficult to face. I'm not the sort of person who gives up on something just because it's hard to do. I'm a Dingle, and Dingles keep their word (on the whole). So I'm going to write down the truth and the whole truth . . .

Mandy's Secret Diary

Mandy Dingle

Edited by Lance Parkin

GRANADA

First published in Great Britain in 2000
by Granada Media, an imprint of André Deutsch Limited
in association with Granada Media Group
76 Dean Street
London
W1V 5HA
www.vci.co.uk

A catalogue record for this book is available from the British Library

ISBN 0 233 99935 3

Cover photographs of Lisa Riley as Mandy Dingle,
reproduced courtesy of Scope Features

Typeset by
Derek Doyle & Associates, Liverpool
Printed in the UK by
Mackays of Chatham plc, Chatham, Kent

1 3 5 7 9 10 8 6 4 2

The Diary

Tuesday 11 July

I've never kept a diary before. OK, I did once, at primary school – every Monday morning Miss Stonier made us write down what we did at the weekend. So I put everything down in black and white. I wrote about trying to fix a horse race, or being entered for a beauty contest and winning £10 prize money, or hitching a lift on a dustbin lorry to go to a wedding in the middle of a field in Shropshire. Miss Stonier used to say I had a great imagination and my stories were very funny, so she didn't mind me making them up. I never had the heart to tell her that every word of it was true.

That's what it's like being a Dingle. No one ever believes us.

I'm writing a diary now because of my cousin, Butch. He died back in March, in a bus crash. Hardly anyone knew Butch Dingle. He was big, I mean big even for a Dingle, which is huge. He had a skinhead cut, years before David Beckham made them trendy.

He didn't say very much. And when people saw him, they saw a big thick lout.

And sometimes Butch <u>was</u> a big thick lout. A few years ago he pretty much stalked a girl called Sophie. Sophie had encouraged him a bit at first, but then she'd made it clear she wasn't interested. As clear as she could – she became a lesbian and started going out with Zoe Tate instead. Butch didn't take the hint. He followed Sophie around, threw bricks through windows. Zoe never forgave him. Last year, long after she and Sophie had split up and Sophie had left the village, Zoe moved back into Home Farm and the first thing she did was to sack Butch from his job as groundsman there, even though he'd been doing a great job.

Butch had a more tender side. Until last year the great loves of Butch's life were a rat – I'm not joking, he called her Jessica – and his pigs. He gave all the pigs names and talked to them when they were sick. Needless to say, Butch's dad, my Uncle Zak, wasn't impressed by this show of affection. You can imagine the sort of jokes Zak came up with. So the people that didn't know Butch thought he was just a thug, and the people that did know him thought he was a simpleton.

But there was more to Butch. Hardly anyone ever saw it. I did, when I was married to him. Yes . . . I was married to Butch, for six months. It's a long story, and you don't really need to know it. The point was that everyone involved knew it was a marriage of convenience – just a bit of paper. Or so I thought. But Butch didn't understand. He'd always had a thing for me, and when we got married, he started to think it might work out between us. Like them romantic novels, where the heroine is forced to marry some bloke against her will, but ends up growing to love him. Butch wasn't one for reading romantic novels, or any sort of books where there were less pictures than pages. But he was a romantic, in his funny kind of way. Family is important to us Dingles, we always want to do things right. Butch wanted the marriage to work. If he was going to be married, he wanted to be properly married. He thought when he had me where he wanted me that I'd come round to his way of thinking.

It would never work. That was obvious to everyone but him. At first I was furious with him. Then we tried to patch things up, and went for a couple of nights out. Bowling, the Diner, that sort of thing. And we talked. It was only then that I realized Butch had hidden depths – extraordinarily well hidden, but they were there. I remember sitting with him in a bus shelter in Hotten one night, waiting to go home. I said something about flowers at funerals. And out of the blue Butch said he didn't want flowers, he wanted people to give the money to charity. He'd thought about it. Realizing then how wonderful he was, I pecked him on the cheek and then the bus came.

Last year Butch started to surprise us with moments like that – sensitive-like – more and more.

Marriage to me, however short-lived, made him grow up a bit. I think the biggest change was Belle. His baby sister, born on Christmas Day 1998, which was nice and festive. He said afterwards that he'd seen plenty of newborn pigs and dogs but this was different. He really loved Belle, took care of her, made sure their dad, Zak, really was a house-husband, not just saying that to skive off. He put most of his earnings in the Belle Jar, the money bank we had so Belle could have all the baby things she needed. He started questioning Uncle Zak's schemes for the first time, he started standing up for himself, and arguing on behalf of his step-mum Lisa, whenever she felt the pressure.

Then he met Emily Wylie. Poor Emily. She's tiny, not much to look at. But she's the most honest person I've ever met. Simple, but not stupid – she has her faith, she believes that people should work hard, she hates fighting, or even loud noises. She always sees the best in people, even horrible people like Viv Windsor and Pollard. She'd lived up on the hills all her life. A sheltered life. Her mum died when she was little, and her dad brought her up strict. The sort of strict you usually only see in fairy tales. She wasn't allowed out very often, and when she was, she had to come straight back. I have to keep reminding myself that I'm younger than Emily – she's so innocent, so sheltered, she sees Emmerdale as the big city. She'd only ever travelled as far as Hotten, eight miles away, and when Butch took her to the pictures in Leeds to see *The Phantom Menace* she treated it like an expedition to Mars. But she's a decent person.

Butch was the first person from the village to talk to her. She had applied to work at the post office and was waiting at the bus stop before her interview. Butch saw she looked worried and lumbered up to her – Butch was like that, it would never have occurred to him that the last thing someone of a nervous disposition needed was a great lump like him looming over her.

And they hit it off. To everyone else in the world, they were both just soft in the head. They were simple, I suppose. Their love was simple. They brought out the best in each other – Emily gave Butch someone to love, something he could understand. Emily told him that violence wasn't the only way to solve problems, that he should think about his future and his responsibilities.

To the outside world, we were all still just the Dingles, marrying our cousins, getting evicted, pulling scams, on the rob. Larger than life. A joke. But the Dingles are a proper family, we love each other, we stay loyal. There's not many people in Emmerdale can say that. When I look at Chris Tate and Sean Reynolds, I see real criminals, however big their houses are, however often they say how important their kids are to them. They killed Butch, and they got away with it. They skimped on their repair bills at the haulage yard, the brakes on one of their lorries failed, and it crashed into a bus Butch was on.

Butch was in hospital for a week, but the doctors all but said straight away that there was no hope. Emily sat by the bedside the whole time. She married him on his deathbed, both of them knowing that it was the right thing to do. When Butch died, Emily was with him. The others waited outside.

So Butch is dead. I don't think even his dad knew what was going on in his head half the time. He'd make a joke of it, say there was room for a concert in there. Lisa, I think, talked to Butch a few times, I did, like I said. Emily knew him, she drew things out of him, shared his innermost thoughts. In twenty-seven years, I think Emily was the only person who ever knew what my cousin was really like.

My dad's been ill for a long time. It's serious, that much is obvious. He's not that old, but he's had heart problems for a while and he had a rough time of it last year: he fell off a church roof, which didn't help, and before he'd recovered from that he managed to break his ankle. It all adds up, and Dad's in a bad way. Of course, in the tried and trusted Dingle manner, he doesn't suffer in silence. When it comes to illness there are two types of people – those who stay in their bedrooms and keep quiet until they're better, and those who sit in the middle of the front room so everyone in the house knows just how ill they are, and who make sure that everyone has to work round them if they want to get anything done. Dad's definitely the latter. But I think this time that it is serious. He'll pull through, but it's not like he can just pick himself up and dust himself off like he used to.

People die, don't they? I try to think about people I've known who've died. Rachel Hughes – all I can remember really is her frizzy hair, that she was good at running and she looked after Zak and Butch when we were all evicted. Is that fair? I doubt she'd be flattered. Graham Clark – I remember him being dead nice, a bit boring even, but it turns out he killed Rachel, and his first wife, and he died trying to murder Kathy Glover. And people round Emmerdale still have the nerve to judge the Dingles by their appearance. I keep telling people it's always the quiet ones, and if that's the case, I know I'm in the clear.

I don't want to be morbid, but what would people remember about me if I died? I'm not like Butch – I've never had a problem expressing my feelings, I've opened my heart to all sorts of people over the years, I've had a lot of good friends. Kelly Glover knows a lot about me. My husband Paddy does. Zak and Lisa. But there are some things that no one knows about me. I know how people would remember me: they'd think of leopardskin tops and a big gob. They'll remember me being dragged away by the bailiffs or punching Pollard, or wrestling with Tricia Stokes in the mud behind the Woolpack. But that's not me at all. That's not all I am.

This evening, I saw a box full of year 2000 diaries

at Hotten Radio. Giveaways, I assume. I'm sure they won't miss one of them, especially now it's July. I'll try and write something every day – I can't promise that I'll be able to absolutely every day, but I'll give it a try.

So, here's where I'll write it all down. The untold story, the secret diary of Mandy Dingle. The real me.

Thursday 13 July

Perhaps I am psychic. Perhaps my horoscopes really do work.

I was thinking about my dad yesterday, and how he'd been ill. I just had the feeling something was wrong. This morning Dad phoned and once again he's taken a turn for the worse. You could tell just from his voice on the phone – he was coughing, the effort of talking almost seemed too much for him. I just wanted to get straight down there. I know there's already most of the rest of our clan in the area, but they don't live in the same house now, and he always seems to look forward to his only daughter being there. For the whole of this year, I've been going back and forth to Southampton to look after him. It's been hard on my marriage – I've been away from Emmerdale for months at a time. Paddy's been very understanding, but the last time I had to go, Paddy got annoyed. He asked why he couldn't come first for a change.

I understand, I really do. But Paddy did exactly the same last year, in exactly the same circumstances. His mother told him she was on her deathbed, and Paddy dropped everything – all but abandoned his partnership at the vets. Paddy always was a bit of a mummy's boy, but this was ridiculous. Barbara Kirk is a poisonous old bag, as middle class and awful as that woman off those bog roll commercials. And Paddy had been the perfect son – uneventful adolescence, good exam results, a degree in veterinary medicine. And she didn't even mind he wasn't a doctor – her other son did that. So she didn't need anyone else to look after her, and Paddy could look after her pets. She thought Paddy was second best, and was a bit worried he had never had a girlfriend, so had one lined up for him – Jane, an old school friend. I met her. She's stick thin, she's got a pretty face, and one day there's even the danger she might say or do something interesting.

When Paddy fell for me, Paddy's mum wasn't impressed. People judge us Dingles by appearance, or reputation, or they just look at the criminal record, they don't see the person. I've been to prison a couple of times, but, then, who hasn't? Half of Emmerdale's done time (or managed to hitch a ride on a helicopter so they didn't have to) and the other half should have done. But there's still snobbery about it, like it makes you a bad person. Even though I'm used to that, I wasn't ready for just how

over-the-top Barbara Kirk's reaction was. She didn't
want me anywhere near her son, she didn't want him
living in our barn. She definitely didn't want to be a
Dingle mother-in-law.

And, to cut a long story short, one of the ways she
tried to drive a wedge between me and Paddy was
to fake a terminal illness. She would sit there in bed
in her big house in Harrogate, propped up, make-up
on her face to make herself look pale, coughing
every so often and making Paddy run downstairs for
glasses of water. She said she'd got a weak consti-
tution, and she couldn't stand the stress of having
me around. And when that worked, and Paddy was
spending every evening with her instead of me, she
started on the next stage: it was no good – even
though she never saw me, she couldn't get me out of
her mind. The mere thought of me was enough to
bring her out in hives, whatever they are.

And Paddy was really upset. When her doctor told
Paddy she was dying, that she only had a few
months to live, Paddy was devastated. Jane was
around at the time – she was a family friend, and
she was around for Paddy to talk to.

And I was upset too. I love Paddy – whatever I
think of Barbara the Bag, I wouldn't wish her dead.
My mum died when I was young, and I wouldn't wish
that on anyone. And if she only had a few months to
live . . . well, I didn't want there to be any bad blood
between us. So I went to Harrogate, I took Kelly
Glover with me. Well, she was Kelly Windsor back

then. Back then she was a good friend, too.

Anyway.

We went to her house. It was massive. Houses in the Dales are worth a lot of money. Rich people buy them as holiday homes, or weekend cottages. A lot of people commute to Leeds. Emmerdale's in a beautiful part of the country – so you can understand why people snap them up. It means folk like me and Kelly, people whose family and friends live here, can't always afford even a little terrace. But houses in Harrogate are <u>dead</u> expensive. Especially houses like Paddy's mum's place. But Barbara wasn't in her lovely house . . . it turned out Barbara was at a fancy gym. And it wasn't physiotherapy. Me and Kelly went there and we saw her, tanned and bouncing around a treadmill like she was ready to do the Great North Run. She'd been faking it all the time. That <u>cow</u> tricked her own son into thinking she was about to die. She'd done it all to keep me and Paddy apart.

Paddy hasn't spoken to her since. She wasn't invited to our wedding. She sent us a Christmas card, but Paddy threw it in the bin. (I rooted it out later – but there wasn't a cheque in it, so I put it back. No harm in checking. Tight cow.)

I reckon Paddy thinks my dad's doing the same thing – faking it to try and split us up. Paddy's been down a couple of times, and he's seen Dad for himself. My dad seemed suspicious. Paddy's very well spoken, very smart, and he was on his best behaviour. That sort of thing doesn't impress my dad. So they didn't really get on. But I'm sure my dad likes Paddy – and I know for a fact that while my dad might be a cunning, conniving, lazy and selfish person at times, there's no way he could be as down-right <u>evil</u> as Paddy's mum. But Paddy has his suspicions, and he always looks at me funny when I say I've got to go back down to Southampton.

So I haven't told Paddy I'm going yet. Not exactly. I'm breaking the news to him slowly. Over breakfast I told him that I'd done my horoscope, and that it predicted distant travel for me. He just did that snorting laugh thing he does and said he doesn't believe in horoscopes.

Tomorrow was going to be my last radio show for a while, anyway. I've been doing this pet horoscope thing. When I'm on, apparently their ratings go right up, and my producer thinks I've got a great career ahead of me as a presenter. Radio Hotten have even printed little postcards of me. They're dead arty – me in a nice leopard blouse, leaning on my elbow, smiling and trying to look sophisticated. Before I did my show, they made me sign a load of them, and they get sent out whenever people ask for them. It's like *Live and Kicking* – people finish off their calls to me with 'Oh, and can I have your autograph, Mandy?' It's great being famous!

One of the callers tonight was Tricia. She didn't give her last name, or ask for my autograph, but how many Essex girls are going to be listening to Hotten Radio? She's just started going out with another of

my cousins, Marlon Dingle. Marlon's been mooning
after her for months, everyone but Tricia could see
that. She asked me if it was going to work out. So I
asked her when Marlon's birthday is (I knew already,
of course, it's March the 23rd, the same day Paddy
proposed to me). Trish told me and seemed
delighted, if unsurprised, that Marlon was a Ram.
When she said she was a Gemini – well, the stars
say the relationship's going to be passionate and
long-lasting. And the stars don't lie very often.
Though if you ask me, if you need an astrologer to
tell you whether it's love or not, the chances are that
it isn't. But I'm not going to tell anyone that. So Tricia
went off happy, and I daresay Marlon's got a grin on
his face tonight, too.

That's why I like doing my radio show. It doesn't
do any harm – it reassures people. Paddy thinks it's
all a load of rubbish. But it makes more sense to me
than those vet books of his. I'm sure there are
higher powers controlling our destiny. I'm sure,
somehow, there's a reason for everything that
happens in Emmerdale. So I've enjoyed my stint
trying to bring some support into people's lives.
And I admit that I was upset to announce that
tomorrow's show was my last for a while, and that
the regular radio vet was going to be back as
normal next week.

And then I told Paddy about Dad. He wasn't happy
– I didn't think he was going to be. He didn't seem
convinced by the argument that it was all pre-

ordained and in the stars. But, to be fair to him, he could see how much it meant to me.

I am really worried about my dad.

Tuesday 18 July

Paddy whinged a bit that I was spending my last evening at Radio Hotten, rather than with him, but I persuaded him that I couldn't let down my fans. In the event, I strayed a bit from the subject matter during the show. Tricia phoned up again, and said that I'd been right about her Ram. After that, a few more hopeful couples rang up, and I did what I could to reassure them. I think I gave them one of Uncle Zak's racing tips, but by then it was a bit of a blur, to be honest and my mind was elsewhere. A load of my listeners rang in to say how much they were going to miss me. I thought that was really sweet and I promised that I would be back. Paddy was my last caller, and he said he was going to miss me most of all, and that was quite sweet, too.

So, after that, it was home, a kiss goodbye from Paddy (I really appreciated the effort he was going to) and then I was off to the coach station at Hotten. Every time I go, I always think it's a really boring journey. It seems to zigzag all over the country (I'm sure you go to Doncaster twice), and the coach is always packed. You go through London, but manage to avoid every single one of the sights.

I'm getting used to going to Southampton, now. It's where Dad and his branch of the Dingle family live. People often say they come from a big family – they don't know the meaning of the word. There are branches of the Dingle family tree everywhere in the world, you're more likely to see a Dingle in a town than a branch of McDonald's. We can trace our ancestry back further than the Queen.

When I got off the coach, I was already homesick. I was a city girl once, but Emmerdale's my home, now. Southampton was all so flat, the air smelt of the sea, there were gulls hopping around a litter bin, pecking at a packet of chips someone had thrown away. If you live in the Dales, the rest of the country, however beautiful it is really, however many tourists take a holiday there, feels so noisy and dirty.

It was getting dark. The coach had arrived ten minutes earlier than scheduled, so I was worried I was going to be left high and dry, but Job was there to meet me. Job Dingle (it's pronounced Jo-buh, like the Bible, not Job like the Centre) is my cousin – Zebediah's (that's my dad's youngest brother) youngest son. He's seventeen, now. He reminds me of Shaggy from *Scooby-Doo*, he's even got that bit of fluff on his chin that teenagers think is a beard. He doesn't live with Dad – Dad's on his own now, as all his clan moved out. There's still a Dingle contingent in and around Southampton, but there's no one in Dad's house. I'm still not 100 per cent on who's still living in the area. Dad and Job, obviously. Job lives on the other side of town now, with my step-brother, Frampton. Fram's son, Key, lives with them, but his mum left a year or two back. I think Fram's twin brother Mungo is still staying there, too. But, like everywhere else Dingles congregate, the roll call keeps changing as people drift around, marry and go in and out of prison. Over the years, we've all left home – me and all four of my step-brothers. Oddly enough, I don't think Dad minds. I think he's got to the age where he enjoys the peace and quiet, and where having a load of teenagers playing their CDs all day and night would just be annoying.

The family visit, they pop in to make sure he's OK, and they use his house as somewhere to lie low and stash stuff, but there's no one willing or able to look after him full-time. Are they being selfish? I've spoken to them, and they've got their own lives – if you've got a kid of your own, you have less time to look after anyone else.

And it's a bit selfish of me, I suppose, to feel annoyed that every few months I've got to come down here. I don't see why the rest of the family should bear the burden just because I live a long way away.

'Hullo, Mandy,' Job said. 'I've got wheels, now, I'll drive us to Caleb's place.'

He pointed at the car parked at an angle on the pavement. The passenger door was maroon, the rest of it was lime green. The interior had those funny bead seat covers.

'What sort of car's that?' I asked sceptically.

He patted the bonnet, but I noticed he was careful not to pat it too hard. 'This bit's a Capri, the back's from a Granada. I call it a Granpri, like them car races.'

'You built it?'

Job went red. 'All me own work.'

I asked him if it was legal.

'Nah,' he said, cheerfully, 'and that means no one will insure it, so I save a bit of money there, too, like.'

It was surprisingly roomy inside, uncluttered by things like a dashboard or seatbelts. Most cars have one car stereo, this one had two. Neither of them worked. Job went through an odd key-waggling ritual to get the car to start.

'How's me dad?' I asked, once the car was moving.

'Oh, you know, he's just Caleb.'

'He's ill, isn't he?'

'Suppose. He doesn't get out of bed unless he has to. But if that's ill, then half the Dingles in the world are ill.'

Dad's a city Dingle. He lives in a house in Southampton and, like him, the house has seen better days. The place looks like it has been spruced up since the last time I was here. Job couldn't confirm or deny it, but thought the council might have been around a few weeks ago to cut the grass and sort out the drains.

If the council had been, they certainly didn't make it over the doorstep. The hall is full of junk, as usual – a suspicious number of bikes, a statue that looks like it's garden furniture, bits of car engine which Job had presumably not found a place for when he'd been putting his Granpri back together. The walls are that murky yellow that only decades of chain smoking can achieve.

Job didn't bother going to see Dad; he seemed more interested in the carburettor he spotted on the pile of junk. I went upstairs, bracing myself for the worst. Every time I've been to see Dad, it's been a shock to see just how bad a way he's in. This time, though, it was a pleasant surprise. Dad lay on the bed, while little Keanu read the *Racing Post* to him. Key was Dad's first grandchild. He was six now, and his teachers were very impressed by his reading age, his knowledge of horses and his grasp of spread betting.

'Hello, Auntie Mandy,' Key squeaked.

I ruffled his hair. 'Hiya.'

'Hello there, Mandy love.'

Dad looks much better than last time. He was propped up in bed in a dressing gown that was several sizes too big for him, surrounded by sweet wrappers. The room was full of cigarette smoke. I gave them the racing tip I'd come up with on my radio show. Dad frowned and looked over to Key, who was also frowning.

'Mercury's in the ascendant, so it's a sure thing,' I assured them.

Dad shrugged. 'Worth a tenner, I suppose. Key?'

The lad was already scurrying away.

'He goes back to school in a couple of weeks, I don't know what I'll do, then.'

'That better not be why you sent for me.'

He managed a weak smile. 'Mandy, love, I'm not well.'

'I know that,' I told him. He didn't look well.

'Doctors say it's ~~emfeeseema emphes~~ emphysema.'

If Paddy had been with me, he'd have told me what that was. I forgot to ask when I phoned him up to tell him I'd arrived safely. That's the other advantage of having a diary, I can write little notes to myself like this. Ask Paddy about emphysema.

'Smoking,' Dad explained. 'It's to do with me lungs. Not cancer, but not good, either.'

My heart was sinking. Dad had always been a bit accident prone, but he just got back up, dusted himself off and carried on. But this time he hadn't got back up.

'Are you going to be OK?' I asked, not wanting to know the answer.

'Don't worry, Mandy love, I'm not going to peg it this evening. But I may not make it, I may need a transplant, it could get worse. The doctors aren't sure just yet.'

He looked very pink-faced, and just sitting up and

talking to me had left him short of breath. Perhaps he wasn't as well as I thought at first.

'What is it?' I asked. 'I mean how do you get it? Smoking?'

He nodded.

I've never smoked, and that makes me pretty unusual for a Dingle – Zak and Marlon smoke. I'd never seen the appeal of paying to give myself a disease. Seeing my dad like that, I'm not going to start now, either. I wondered whether Zak and Marlon would give up if they saw my dad like this, all pink and puffing, with his chest a funny shape.

Probably not.

I'd only just noticed a big gas cylinder propped up on the other side of the bed. I thought at first it was one of those blowtorches – oxyacetylene ones. Cutting gear. Lisa used to have one at the garage, and Zak was always going on about how he'd have to borrow it – he reckoned you could get through any safe or strongbox. Lisa vetoed the idea, of course – and the chances are, Zak would have ended up welding shut whatever it was he was planning to break into. But this stuff was clean, shiny and new, and there were all sorts of tubes coming off it, and little plastic masks and dials.

Dad saw me looking at it. 'That's what I need, now,' he said. 'It's my oxygen therapy.' It really brought home that Dad was ill, and that this was something new and scary. They wouldn't give him one of those if it wasn't serious, would they?

I must have looked horrified, because he made a reassuring face. 'Oh, don't worry, I don't need it all the time. Just if I wear myself out. And sometimes if I'm having a rough time sleeping. It's expensive kit is that. I tried flogging it, but there's no market for it.'

'And you know how to use it?'

'Yeah, well, it's really not that difficult to get the hang of it. You just turn a few dials and stick that mask on your face.'

We talked. He'd gone into hospital a few weeks ago for a few routine tests – he's been in and out of hospital since he fell off that roof, as various complications kept cropping up. The doctor spotted that Dad was getting out of breath, and decided to check his breathing. Following that, he got worried, and booked Dad into a specialist. Of course, they didn't really tell him what the problem was ('No need to worry you'), and Dad's not exactly good at dealing with authority, so he didn't push. But he turned up for the test a week later (you'd think the speed of that would have been enough to tip him off that something serious was up – since when do you only have to wait a week on the NHS?). They ran some tests, and there and then, they told him that he was seriously ill.

They needed to do a full report and do some checking, that sort of thing, but they told him there was clearly something up with his breathing, and that his lung capacity was really well below what they'd expect. Then they asked him if he had any questions.

Dad laughed. 'I said I had: did they have a ciga-rette?'

I looked at him sadly. Broken bones, even a bit of heart trouble, I can deal with that – but this really scares me. This is stuff catching up with him. I'm not sure what I can do – if there really is anything I can do.

Wednesday 19 July

I didn't sleep well. I was tired, but I was so worried about Dad.

Usually when I get down to Southampton, seeing him is reassuring – Caleb's still Caleb, like Job said yesterday. He bounces back, he always seems inde-structible. You think that about your parents, don't you? That they'll always be there, and they'll always be able to sort out any problems they've got. And every other time, Dad's lived up to that – I've been here a couple of weeks and, at the end of it, he's up and about again, mended.

I had to make myself breakfast. Dad wasn't up, and I didn't want to wake him. As soon as he was up, I planned to make it for him. After all, Dad couldn't cope on his own, and there was only me to look after him, wasn't there? You'd think so, wouldn't you?

The doorbell rang at eight. I thought it must be the

postman. I was still in my dressing gown, and I was a bit worried the toaster wasn't popping properly, so I didn't really want to go in case I burnt my toast – or, if the fault was more serious, the house burnt down. But it's not like Dad could make his way downstairs, so I went. I opened the door and I met Neil. He didn't introduce himself at first. He just sort of looked at me like I was the last thing he was expecting. Seriously – for two or three seconds he just stood with his mouth open. I pulled my dressing gown tight, and glared at him.

'You've got the wrong house,' I told him. 'Unless you're from the Lottery.'

He took the hint.

'Hi, sorry. I'm Neil.'

'Neil?' I said, and I hope he realized from the way I said it that I'd got no idea who 'Neil' was. He paused for a moment, like he was expecting it to all fall into place and me to say 'Ah, Neil, of course, come in.'

I didn't.

'Are you Amanda?' he asked.

'I'm Mandy.'

'Oh, I thought you were Amanda, Caleb's daughter.'

'Mandy's short for Amanda,' I explained to him, a great deal more patiently than I was feeling.

He blushed. 'Sorry, I'm being really thick this morning.'

I know I said it's wrong to judge people by appearances, I know you shouldn't reach snap decisions about people. But I knew straight away that Neil's a wally. He is absolutely nowt to look at. He's got no dress sense. He wears grey slacks, for heaven's sake. When he walks, it's like he's not quite sure how to. I'm sure his mum cuts his hair. And he's got one of them Southern accents, the sort that get right on my nerves.

'Can I come in?' he said.

'Who are you?' I asked, and the way I said it obviously shocked him.

'I'm your dad's carer,' he explained.

I looked at him. 'My dad's not got a carer.'

'I've been coming for two months.'

I was still wondering if he'd got the wrong house. Statistically, the chances of it being a different Caleb on the same street were pretty remote. So when you work out how likely it was that this other Caleb needed daycare and had a daughter who Neil hadn't met called Amanda . . . well, if you had a horse at that odds, you'd shoot it, not bet on it.

'You come round every day to check on him?'

'Typical Caleb,' he laughed. 'I'm here from eight until six every day and he doesn't even mention me to his daughter.'

Suddenly this sounded all too possible.

Key was arriving, with a bag full of stuff.

'Has he been sending you on errands again, Keanu?' Neil said sternly.

Key nodded, clearly worried. 'I fort I'd get here before you did,' he admitted.

'Well, you didn't,' Neil said sternly.

I told Neil to leave him alone.

Neil reached into Key's shopping bag and pulled out a packet of cigarettes. Neil scowled. 'I can't believe the shop sold you these.'

'They ain't for me, they're for Caleb.'

Neil put them in his pocket. 'Caleb can't have them.'

I didn't like this. Don't get me wrong – Key shouldn't have been buying cigarettes, and Dad shouldn't be smoking them. But who was Neil to stop him?

I asked him that question once Key was on his way. Neil smiled at me, shook his head and stepped inside like he owned the place.

'Do you want a coffee?' he asked. 'Oops – I can smell toast burning.'

Once I'd sorted that out and opened the kitchen window, I went upstairs and got dressed. By the time I was ready, Neil was already in with Dad, giving him a cup of coffee.

It reminded me of a Carry On film – Neil was fussing around Dad like a matron. The things he was saying were so patronizing, and the tone of voice as he plumped up Dad's pillows, opened up the curtains and checked the setting on the oxygen cylinder – it was like my dad was six years old.

Dad lapped it up.

'You didn't even mention me to Amanda, did you?' Neil scolded.

Dad chuckled.

'How long has he been coming?' I asked.

Neil butted in. 'I told you, Amanda, two months.'

I ignored him.

'And he's here all day?'

Dad looked cocky. 'At night sometimes, when it's been bad. I'd prefer a blonde in a nurse's uniform, but they said I could only do that if I went private.'

Neil smiled at Dad's joke. They both looked so smug.

'Then why am I here?' I asked.

Dad and Neil looked puzzled.

So I explained to them exactly how difficult it was to just leave Emmerdale at a moment's notice. How inconvenient it was for everyone, how it meant I'd already lost my job at the Woolpack because Bernice couldn't rely on me being there when I said I would be, and how it was a strain on me and Paddy.

'Don't you want to care for your old dad?' my dad asked.

I told him I wasn't going to give in to emotional blackmail. I love him, and I've proved that by dropping everything and coming down here for weeks at a time.

Neil told him that he could give my dad expert care. But when I asked him, Neil admitted that he wasn't a doctor.

'I know a bit of first aid,' he admitted. 'And I've borrowed a book from the library about emphysema.'

'Is that right?' I replied. 'Read a book? You're practically Doug Ross, then, aren't you?'

Neil said he didn't know who Doug Ross was. I told my dad that if Neil didn't even watch *ER*, then I probably knew more about medical treatment than Neil did.

Dad laughed. 'She's married to a pig doctor and so she thinks she knows all about it now.'

'You're married?' Neil asked.

Dad told him all about Paddy. The Dingle version, anyway – how Paddy's posh and comes from a family that thinks marrying a Dingle is beneath them, and how he'd rather spend money on himself than spend it on his family, and how he looks after pigs.

'He's a pig farmer?'

'He's not a pig farmer, he's a vet,' I told them both wearily. 'He went to university, he studied veterinary medicine. He's been a vet for years, and now he's the partner of a vet's surgery.'

'And after all that hard work, he still spends all day stood in a muddy field with his hands up sheep,' Dad laughed. 'There's a lesson there, Neil.'

Neil pretended to look impressed. Dad gave that smug little smile of his.

'I might not watch *ER*, but I used to like *All Creatures Great and Small*. I know there's more to being a country vet than Caleb's saying. You're from Herriot country, aren't you? Didn't they used to film it up there?'

I wasn't standing for this.

27

'You're not needed,' I told Neil. 'I'll look after him.'

'I'm here because the social ser—'

'I don't care why you're here. I'm here to look after my dad. I don't need help.'

'Your father is ill and—'

'He's been ill before. I looked after him before.'

Dad smiled. 'You won't talk her round, Neil. Why don't you just take the day off? Call it a holiday, come back in a day or so to check up on us.'

Neil considered this.

I stared at him very hard and stood my ground. I thought it might help his decision.

'Mandy's not the sort to lose arguments, Neil,' Dad laughed.

Neil looked at me, and buckled.

Coward.

'I'll be back tomorrow,' he assured Dad.

'There's no need,' I told him.

He went away. Good riddance.

When I'd made sure Neil was gone, things got back to normal. Into the routine I was used to from before. When dad was up, and safely installed in his armchair, watching *House Invaders*, I asked him how my horse had got on – if it came up, I wanted a cut of the profits.

Dad gave one of those smiles of his. 'Mandy, love, by the time the race had finished, I wasn't even sure it <u>was</u> a horse.'

'That bad?'

He nodded, gave a great coughing laugh, and

went back to watching Anna Ryder Richardson. She was redecorating a bathroom, saying she wanted it to have a Moroccan feel.

'I wouldn't mind her giving me a Moroccan feel,' Dad said, giving a mucky laugh.

He'd just blanked Neil from his mind, I'm sure. After Neil had gone, Dad didn't even mention him. But Neil's obviously been coming around, so why did he need me? Neil obviously wasn't doing a good enough job.

So if that horse didn't win, perhaps I can't see into the future, after all. A shame that, it would come in dead handy. But then, if astrologers could really predict stuff, they'd be rich wouldn't they? That's what Paddy always says – 'If Russell Grant's really that good, why doesn't he just make himself rich?' I saw his big house on *Through the Keyhole*, once. I don't think Russell Grant's done too bad for himself.

I did my horoscope, just to see what it said my future would bring. I don't get the sense that I'm the vessel for vast celestial powers, or I'm channelling the spirit world, or anything, but when I do a chart and come up with stuff I'm usually right at least as often as I'm wrong, and that can be a bit freaky. So, what does Mystic Mandy predict?

I'm going to be presented with a great choice.

That's it. Nothing else.

Judging on the evidence of today, that seems pretty unlikely – I had precisely two choices today: Dad let me choose whether I wanted to watch the

Lottery or *Ainsley's Barbecue Bible*; and I had to decide whether I wanted vinegar or not on the chips I got from the takeaway. I imagine my choices tomorrow will be about the same.

So much for the stars.

Thursday 20 July

Neil's dedicated, I'll give him that. I didn't expect him to come back. He rang the bell at eight this morning, and he was cheerful with it. This time I was already dressed. I wasn't expecting him, I just happened to be up and about.

'Is it OK if I come in?' he said.

I'd never admit it, but it was. I always forget what a pain Dad can be. Half an hour after Neil had gone, I really wished there was someone there to run errands for Dad. He'd ask me to go and fetch something from downstairs, but wouldn't say where it was. Then he'd say he didn't mean he wanted that, he meant something else. Then by the time I'd found what he wanted, he'd decided he didn't want to do that after all, and went to sleep for an hour.

If he was ten years older, I'd have thought he was getting forgetful, like old people do. But he's not. He's sharp as a button, whatever that expression is supposed to mean. He jokes, he can tell you what's been happening to all the various members of the

Dingle family (it's like a quiz – give him a name or a place, and he can just reel off an update), he can get seven-letter words on *Countdown*, that sort of thing.

Dad knows exactly what he's doing. He wants to be the centre of attention, he wants everyone to know who's boss, and he wants everything that happens to revolve round him. In a packed house like Zak's place, or like Dad used to run before we all moved out, we'd all take turns, the burden would be shared. But now it's only me.

The worst thing is that Dad doesn't thank me for it. I've travelled hundreds of miles to be with him, to look after him, and he just takes it for granted. I know it's not the Dingle way, but saying 'thank you' just once wouldn't hurt him.

No: the worst thing is that Dad really is ill. I must sound so selfish. But I'm upset, too. My dad is dying, and there's no one there to look after <u>me</u>. I get lonely. I don't like waking up on my own, knowing that I hardly know anyone down here, that all my friends are going about their business without me. I think part of the problem is that I'm a lot like my dad. I want to be the centre of attention, but it's not like I can be the life and soul of the party here. When I think like that, I feel selfish again. Whatever I'm going through, it's nothing like as serious as what Dad's going through.

So, relief that Neil's here. It means I can get a few minutes off, it means my dad's got someone else to pick on. It means he can't bully us very much, now there are two other people here – he's back on his best behaviour. A problem shared is a problem halved and all that. If Neil wants to run around after my dad for no thanks and less money than he'd get working in McDonald's, then I'm not going to stop him.

Neil seems to have forgotten yesterday's row. He's obviously not the sort of person that bears grudges. He must be quite a weak person. Being selfless and charitable is a good thing to be, obviously, but I get the feeling with Neil that he's doing it because he can't do anything else. I don't know how old he is, but he's got to be thirty-five, at least. He's not married (he doesn't have a ring). By his age – well, you should have <u>achieved</u> something, yeah? Neil's just boring. Enough about Neil.

Dad can walk OK. He gets out of breath when he climbs the stairs (they're steep stairs and there's quite a lot of them. I get out of breath, to be honest). He's not an invalid. I rang Paddy, and he said emphysema means you lose a lot of lung capacity – from what I could tell him, he reckons Dad's lost about half the use of his lungs. So breathing's difficult and he gets out of breath easily. Paddy said it was quite serious, but he could tell that the doctors had made sure he was getting the right treatment. I asked him whether he'd ever treated emphysema. Paddy laughed. Cows don't get it, apparently. He promised to have a word with his brother, and also to look it up and he'll report back to me in the next couple of days. All credit to Paddy: he didn't hassle me about coming back to Emmerdale after that. I didn't tell Paddy about Neil. He'd only ask why I had to be down here when Dad's already got someone caring for him.

So why am I still here? Dad needs someone around him he can trust. Neil's not the same. He's not family. He's one of those outsiders, the people that don't get past appearances. He probably goes back to . . . not his wife . . . possibly his boyfriend. No. His mum. He goes back to his mum and says 'Oh, I spent another day with those funny Dingles'.

So what are my days like at the moment? They revolve around Dad. I get to go to the shops (with Dad telling me what he wants me to pick up on the way out – but, funnily enough, never offering to pay for any of it). I've managed to go on the city walls, and have a look at the ships or boats or whatever they are. I did a bit of clothes shopping. Window shopping, of course. Dad gets up about ten and comes down to sit in his chair. On nice days, like today, he sits in the garden. But he can't keep running about for things. He can't go to the shops and going up and down the stairs is a big deal (they're talking about getting a stairlift, like Chris Tate has). He doesn't need a wheelchair, but Neil reckons he might one day.

I talk to Dad, tell him about things that have been going on in Emmerdale – like my radio show. I ask him what's been happening here, but he hardly ever tells me, and when he does it's dead boring. 'There's no death and disaster here,' he says.

Monday 24 July

Neil's going to be trouble. He thinks he knows what's best. And what he thinks is best for Dad is so insulting – when he talks to him, it's like he's talking to a child. He won't let Dad do anything. It quickly got to the stage where we were being petty with each other – Neil would open the curtains, and I'd go straight over and close them again. I'd bring him his lunch, and Neil would cut it up for him. That's right – cut the food up, like he didn't think Dad could be trusted to use a knife and fork.

And Neil's so picky – don't sit there . . . don't you think you should . . . don't shout, it'll only upset him. 'That's right, isn't it, Caleb?' he says. He says it all the time. Every time Neil does something that I disagree with, he leans over my dad and says 'That's right, isn't it Caleb?' in that soft Southern poncey voice of his. Imagine the most patronizing, sing-song voice you can – that's what Neil sounds like.

Dad laughed at us. 'You're like an old married couple,' he told us. He thinks it's a joke. I half-suspect he's got me down to Southampton just so he can watch me squabble with Neil. I wouldn't put it past him. Like all the Dingles, he likes a good argument.

Neil goes at six, so I'm stuck in the house in the evenings. It's like being fourteen again, with my dad sat in the same chair, watching the same terrible programmes. I got flashbacks when he told me I couldn't watch *Top of the Pops*, he wanted to watch some rubbish on the other side. My dad's asleep by ten. I have to help him upstairs, not that he'll admit it. And I go to the spare bedroom. The mattress has a label on it 'Property of HMP Parkhurst'. When I asked him, Dad told me that Frampton had liberated it the last time he was released. He was vague on quite how you could walk out of prison with a mattress (and half a set of cutlery, it turns out) under your arm. But Frampton always had initiative.

Lisa phoned to say that she's on speaking terms with Kathy again, after the burglary, and Kathy's even offered to pay for the work Lisa and Jason did at the house. Lisa was decorating for Kathy, and had her keys. There was no sign of a break-in at the house, and so the police saw Lisa's name was 'Dingle', and assumed she'd done it. She hadn't, of course.

OK, it was Cain. So there was a Dingle involved – but he was acting on his own, and Zak sorted him out: Kathy's been good to us over the years. She's been the one campaigning the hardest to see Tate Haulage punished for the bus crash. She was injured herself, but she's always kept in touch with us about Butch, made sure that we knew what was going on, checked to make sure the Dingles didn't mind her using

Butch's name and picture on her placards. So us Dingles should be looking out for Kathy, not robbing her. Cain's been put right by Zak, and the necklace has magically reappeared. I told Dad, and he was furious with Cain – he was on the phone to Shadrach (Cain's dad, his brother) as soon as he could get to it.

Dad fumed for the rest of the night about the Dingle Code, and how the younger generation had forgotten their duties. He seemed to include me in that. Dad doesn't seem to distinguish between Cain robbing our friends and me dropping everything to help him. Which doesn't annoy me, it just makes me feel depressed – why bother, if my own dad just lumps me in with a thug like Cain?

The spare bedroom is small, with bare walls and a tiny window. It's my third night here, and I've not even stepped out of the house since I arrived. Somehow, sleeping on a prison mattress doesn't seem inappropriate.

Tuesday 25 July

I thought I was imagining it, but they showed Emmerdale on the telly tonight – footage of the aftermath of the air crash. A Concorde crashed in France, and the news haven't got pictures yet, so they're using old pictures of the last time this sort of thing happened. Everyone in the village who was there must have had a terrible reminder of what it was like. Ashley will call a special prayer service, I'm sure. I wish I was in the village to offer my support.

I miss Emmerdale, I'm homesick.

It always hits me about a week after I get down here. It starts even before I wake up. I try to cuddle up to Paddy, but he's not there. And I wake up, and I remember that he's on the other side of the country, with all my friends, and Uncle Zak and Lisa and just about everything and everyone I know. Then there's the dawn chorus. In Emmerdale, there are normal birds. Sparrows and starlings and those other brown ones that I don't know the name of. Here it's a bunch of seagulls, real foghorn squawks and screeching. It gets light earlier, too, and the light's not as warm and friendly as it is in the Dales, it's that harsh light that comes reflected off the sea. The buildings here are all boarding houses and villas. There are worse places than Southampton, but there are few better than Emmerdale. I just miss the Dales cottages in limestone with their high roofs. I miss the hills.

With Dad being housebound, I don't even get to take advantage of the night-clubs in the evenings. They're meant to be dead good these days, and leaflets for them keep being posted through the letter-box – there are about a dozen of them, as far as I can tell. There are a couple of big cinemas, too. All I get to see of them are those flyers and adverts and reviews in the local paper. Emmerdale is not exactly noted for its night-life or multiplex cinema – the nearest we get to that is Seth playing the piano in the Woolpack Bar for you if you buy him a pint. So I wouldn't normally miss it. But here they are tantalizingly close – you can hear them at night.

Not that there's anyone I could take to a night-club or to the pictures – I could always get Trish and Jason and Paddy to go into Hotten (which has more clubs than you'd think). But here, I'd go on my own. And that's pretty sad, really.

Paddy's got used to me ringing first thing. He's an early riser, and he's said over and over again that it's OK for me to ring – 'I'll get up ages before you ever will,' he says. And I think he knows that I have to hear his voice at least once a day to remind me that Emmerdale's still there.

Seth's been hassling Paddy. That tip I gave did come up – at ten to one. I'm the toast of the village, Paddy says – Zak and Seth and quite a few of the others have made a few bob. Seth wants the next tip from me now – Paddy did a great impression of him 'I don't hold with them horryscoops but if it's summat that picks winners then it's all right bah me.' I told Paddy that I'm not sure I could pick another one. Paddy said he knew that – but I had to tell Seth something to get him off his back. I promised I'd sort out something for him. I was going to tell him just to pick a horse from the paper, with a pin, but I didn't want to admit that's what I'd done first time round. Paddy seemed quite impressed that I'd managed to use astrology to divine the winner. He went out of his way to tell me he couldn't see how where Jupiter was in the sky influenced how fast horses ran, but he didn't seem quite so sceptical. It's the first time he's ever admitted it <u>might</u> be true, so I'm not going to say anything. I might win that argument yet, dear diary!

I also promised myself that I would sort out my dad. 'I wasn't even sure it <u>was</u> a horse' indeed. He made a hundred quid off me. And that little urchin Key was in on the scam, too.

I asked Paddy what else was going on in Emmerdale. Lisa's worried about the DETR report into the bus crash. She was the mechanic who was meant to have serviced the brakes on the lorry. So she blamed herself for the death of Butch and the others. It's not her fault and Uncle Zak talked her round – but we all know what the law and people can come up with, we all know that it's people like us that get the blame, not people like the Tates. When there's a train crash, the report always says driver error, it never says that the driver's boss was doing things on the cheap and ignored all the warnings. The DETR report will be looking for someone to blame, and when it comes down to it, it's always easy to blame a Dingle.

Meanwhile, instead of putting themselves through the wringer, like Lisa's doing, Chris and Zoe Tate are up to something with La-de-dah Tara, spending money on a stud farm. Adam's muscling in on the deal – volunteering to be head vet there, or something. Paddy did explain but I didn't really listen. Paddy couldn't work out why Adam's so keen to get in Tara's good books. I don't think it's just her good books that he wants to get into, somehow.

What is it with men and stick-thin birds with posh accents? Apparently, you can never be too rich or too thin (although I have to say neither have been priorities in my life – how about 'you can never be too happy or have too many friends' – they seem like better things to be). But Lady Tara's thin and rich enough for anyone I would have thought. I suppose it's the opposite to having a bit of rough – every bloke wants to be that bloke out of *Lady Chatterley's Lover* showing the upper class crumpet what a real man's like and doing odd things with daisy chains. What's his name? That's it. Every bloke wants to be David Mellor.

There's good news, too. Bernice and Ashley have got engaged. A whirlwind romance, but they'll make a good couple. More than can be said for Terry Woods and my cousin Charity. I've always liked Terry. He's an honest bloke, hard-working. And somehow, everything he does goes wrong. He must think Charity Dingle's a sweet young thing – or if he's found out what it is she does for a living, he's probably come over all protective. He's dead wrong if he does.

I want to be back there, banging some heads together and telling people what's going on. Instead I'm stuck here with a dad who I'm sure is trying to be a little more annoying every day, and a man who keeps saying 'That's right, isn't it, Caleb?'.

I'll go mad if I'm here much longer.

Monday 31 July

I feel so ashamed of myself.

The routine carried on as normal. Neil arrived at eight thirty.

'You're late,' I told him.

'Ally was feeling ill,' he explained. 'I needed to make sure she was OK before she went to nursery.'

Who was Ally? His wife? A girlfriend?

'Your mum?' I asked. I've never checked, but that's still my guess – if ever a man lived with his mother, it's Neil.

Or so I thought.

'My daughter.'

That really took me by surprise. I've spotted that he didn't have a wedding ring, but he'd never mentioned that he had kids. It was then that I realized that although we've spent pretty much all day, every day together for the last couple of weeks that I knew nothing at all about Neil. Just from him listening to me talking to Dad, Neil would know loads about me: all about Paddy and Butch and Uncle Zak and Lisa, Sam, Cain, Charity. All my friends. He'd heard me tell my dad about what I'd been getting up to in Emmerdale. And in return, I'd obviously not even asked him the basics. I'd assumed a lot about him, but never bothered to see if I was right.

'You've got a daughter?'

'A son and a daughter: Ally and Blaine. Ally's five, Blaine's four.'

'So you're married?'

He clammed up then. 'I was,' he said.

He wouldn't say anything else. His wife must have died. And quite recently, too, if he's got a four year old.

I spent the rest of the day looking at Neil in a new light. As we went upstairs together, I realized he wasn't the sad loner I thought he must have been. Perhaps he didn't live with his mum, after all. I wondered what else I'd got wrong about him. And he's got a nice smile, too. Never noticed it before, but when he talked about his kids he had this proud little smile, and you realized there was a bit more to him than you saw at first. It's terrible, but I'd just completely misjudged him.

I was on a train once. OK, I've been on a train more than once, but I remember this time vividly. I was on the train back from Manchester to Hotten, and about three seats in front of me I saw a girl with frizzy red hair. Sally Stanley. She'd made my life hell at school. She was in the year above me and she had this gang. This was like when I was nine or ten, I think. Primary School. And this train journey was only three or four years ago. We went to different big schools, so it was ten or twelve years since I'd last seen her.

But I still hated her on sight.

Back in school, she called me names, she started spreading rumours about me, and going on about how my parents were dead poor. And Dingles don't tell on people. So for a year I put up with this, all the taunts you can imagine. You probably know that the cruellest people on earth are ten-year-old girls. I hated Sally Stanley.

So for an hour, as the train wound its way round the Pennines, I glared at the back of her head, tried to beam my thoughts at her. Ninety minutes of me sending wave after wave of hatred. All the worst things you can think of – I thought them, bundled them up and transmitted them straight to her brain. I saw her shiver a couple of times, she even looked round once (I ducked behind the chair in front). Then at Halifax, she stood up. And it wasn't Sally Stanley. It was just this woman with frizzy red hair. She wasn't even the right age. She was thirty-five, at least. Right sort of build, the same sort of haircut (but, c'mon, I thought afterwards – the same haircut Sally Stanley had had in 1986). As she walked past, I grabbed her arm.

'I'm sorry,' I said.

The woman looked down at me. 'What for?' she asked.

And, of course, I couldn't answer. I don't think I've ever felt so ashamed. That poor woman. Who was I being spiteful to except myself? I don't feel quite that bad about Neil. But I've misjudged him. And after I wrote all that stuff when I started my diary about how I shouldn't judge people by appearances.

I resolved to make it up to Neil. From that point on, I would ask him about his life, try to talk through any problems <u>he</u> had, and I'd be sympathetic and be the nice, understanding person I'd like to think I am, not the spiteful person that wanted revenge on Sally Stanley.

The new mood of détente and sympathy for Neil lasted about thirty seconds.

'It's a lovely day, isn't that right, Caleb?'

That <u>voice</u>. I don't know how I can get this across on the page. It's just so irritating. Think of the most irritating voice you can – whether it's a whiny, nasal voice, or a droning, boring one. Everyone hates at least one sort of accent, or those little phrases that people come up with. Like when someone says 'Have a nice day'. I hate that. And – I don't mean any offence – I don't like that posh Southern accent, especially when it's someone not posh and not Southern saying it, someone putting on airs and graces. People shouldn't be ashamed of who they are. I've had this discussion with Zoe and Paddy. Paddy hates it when someone says 'at this moment in time' – because it doesn't mean anything. He says people should just say 'at this moment' or 'now'. Zoe said she hates it when people go on about the Millennium 'really' being January 2001. So think of the accent you find most irritating in the world. Then think of that meaningless, stupid phrase. Then imagine someone saying that phrase in that accent.

That's how irritating Neil is.

As soon as he spoke, I remembered why I'd never asked him about his family or where he lived or what music he liked: he's just so annoying. If he had told me, it would have been in that stupid patronizing voice. And as he went round the room, fussing and faffing, it just annoyed me so much. But Dad seemed to enjoy it.

Dad likes the attention. I asked him about this, when Neil was downstairs, looking for some magazine that my dad had mislaid but now said he couldn't do without.

'I feel like I'm finally winning,' Dad said.

I looked at him, lying in bed, pink-faced, out of breath after just getting out of bed, going to the loo and coming back.

'Winning?'

He smiled. 'The system,' he said. 'All these years, the system's been against us Dingles. They don't like the way the Dingles do business. They don't like people who don't conform. We don't work in offices, we don't take out mortgages and go in for all that rat race.'

And they don't like the way we steal other people's bikes, of course, but Dad didn't mention that.

He carried on: 'And so they find ways to punish us. Just look at Zak's clan.'

'There's nothing wrong with Zak,' I said quickly.

The other Dingles – following Dad's lead – have been suspicious of Zak. He owns the homestead in Emmerdale, now. He had to buy it, because Tara was selling it off. We were all evicted. Lisa and I had to go and live with Betty Eagleton, Zak and Butch kipped on Rachel Hughes' floor at Mill Cottage. But in the end, thanks to Paddy, Zak found the money to buy the house (£6000 – for a huge house, with barns and everything. He got a bargain!). But Dingles don't own their own houses. Half of them don't even rent, they just find a squat. The legal status of my dad's house is best described as 'dodgy' (I don't know all the details, and I'm not sure I want to know). Zak's a homeowner and every other Dingle is worried about that. They think Zak's got ideas above his station. Or worse than that: that he's going soft or bourgeois. The fact he looks after baby Belle while Lisa goes out to work doesn't help. Zak the house-wife, they call him. Not to his face, of course – they know full well that he'd wipe their smug expression off them quick enough.

So Dad sneered at for me leaping in to defend him.

'Look at them,' he said. 'Eviction, prison, people thrown out of work for no reason, they've got Dibble hassling them all the time. It's just because we don't play by their rules. <u>They</u> get suspicious about that. It's the same with Dingles the world over. But now look.'

He tapped that oxygen tank by his bed. 'Free.'

He pointed at the door. 'And they send me Neil. They send me a bloke who'll do anything I say. I want a magazine, he finds it for me. If he can't find it, he apologizes and goes out and buys another one. He cooks for me, does the housework. And at the end of the day I just send him home.'

I shook my head. 'I don't believe you.'

Dad looked at me. 'What have I done now?'

'What have you done? You've got a slave.'

'Hey, less of that.'

I looked at Dad. He'd been rather animated. He'd sat up and waved his arms, and he'd elaborated at great length about the injustices of the system. But he hadn't got out of breath, had he?

Odd that, I thought.

And I told him.

I told Dad that he was a total fraud and that I could see through him. How all the way through his life he'd had people to boss around, but now they'd all left him, so he had to get the council to send one round. But even that wasn't good enough – he had to ruin <u>my</u> life as well. Practically separating me from my husband, making sure I couldn't get any job worth having. Just so he could get to watch me and Neil arguing. And he wasn't really ill. I could see it, even if he'd managed to con every doctor in the Home Counties. I knew that this was just some pathetic scam, a way of getting something he wanted. I'd seen it before – I hadn't taken it from Barbara the Bag, and so there's no way I was going to take it from my own dad.

Dad stared at me for a moment, then looked down, sadly.

'Mandy, how can you possibly think that?' he asked me. I told him how. I told him that I'd seen the way he watched me and Neil arguing. I told him I knew daytime TV was a bit dull, but that in future, he was going to have to settle for watching *Trisha* and the *Teletubbies*. I'd had enough, I was going back home to my husband and my life.

Neil came in. 'I heard shouting. Are you all right, Caleb?' he asked.

I almost hit him.

Instead, I told him that he was an idiot and that if he wanted to help, he could help me pack, but that if he had any sense at all that he should just go now.

And I stormed into my room, threw what few things I'd brought with me into a suitcase and went downstairs.

I'd picked up the phone to phone for a taxi before Neil caught up with me. Neil asked if he could speak to me.

'He's a fraud,' I told him.

'No,' said Neil. And he reminded me of Paddy when he said it. The same soft tone of voice. He was trying to be conciliatory, he was trying to calm me down.

'He's taking advantage of you,' I told him. 'You're too stupid to see that. Or you're just too charitable.

So I told him all about Paddy's mum. I told him what Barbara the Bag had done, and why she'd done it. What she was doing was different – she was doing it to split me and Paddy up. What Dad was doing was just being dead lazy – he didn't want to do the washing up, he didn't want to cook for himself. So he found a way to get a free skivvy.

Neil listened patiently, then asked if that was really what I thought my dad was doing.

I told him I knew him. I'd known Caleb Dingle for twenty-three years. All the Dingles look up to Caleb, I told him. It's not formal, but my dad's the head Dingle. The big godfather Dingle.

'The patriarch,' Neil said.

I told him I did know what a patriarch was, he didn't need to patronize me. And, yes, Caleb Dingle is the patriarch.

What that meant was that he's a Dingle par excellence. People who meet my Uncle Zak, or Ezra, or Albert or any of those others think that they are shifty, or lazy, or cunning or always looking for an angle. When Zak goes into a room, he's always casing it. Always. He goes to the Woolpack and he'll be working out how many nails are keeping the horse brasses on and how much they'd fetch. He goes into a shop, he doesn't see sweets or loaves of bread or CDs, whatever it is the shop sells – he sees job lots of stuff for him to fence. There are two kinds of things – stolen goods and potentially stolen goods.

But Dad would nick 'em. He can't walk past a car without prising off the hubcaps. There's a pile of them in the shed. He doesn't do anything with them – it's not like they're worth 'owt. But he nicks them anyway. It's not even kleptomania. I know it sounds like he's addicted, but it's not. . . <u>compulsive</u>. It's just part of his work ethic. It's what he is, not a problem with what he is.

He's sixty-four years old and he has never done a day's work in his life. Literally not a day's work. Not even a half-day. Even Sam and Butch did some labouring work from time to time, when the family needed the money. 'He's always scamming someone,' I said. 'He's got himself some daycare, but he still needs to get me down, 'cos he knows you go home in the evenings and the TV doesn't have a remote control. You're being conned. Just go home and leave that selfish old man on his own.'

Neil let me say all that, then he told me to sit down. He told me that he'd seen the medical reports for himself. It was serious. 'Caleb's going to die,' he said.

I looked at him. I couldn't say anything.

'When?' I said, at last.

'The doctors don't know,' Neil admitted. 'It could be a couple of years. But he's not going to get any better. The only hope would be a transplant, but he's in a high-risk group, there's a real chance he wouldn't survive the operation.'

'A transplant? A what transplant?'

'Lung,' Neil said. 'It's a routine operation in most cases. It's a big deal, obviously – they need to have the right donor, and that sort of stuff – but they do a lot of them.'

'Does Dad know that?' I asked, when I could think of anything to ask.

'He does.'

I felt terrible. Worse than that. I felt like I had just been told I was going to die.

'I know that Caleb's a colourful character,' Neil said. 'I don't really care what he thinks about me. I think he likes me, deep down. I'm not doing this because I want to be Caleb's friend, I'm doing it because I want to make sure he gets the care he needs. If I didn't . . . I know he's got family. But you have lives of your own. And the only person he really wants here is you. He loves you, Mandy. You know how big his family is, you know how important all this Dingle Law stuff is to him. But of all the people that he could get here by his side, you're the only one he wants to see. He talks about you all the time.'

I can't help myself crying. I . . .

Tuesday 1 August

'Neil told you, didn't he?' Dad asked the next morning.

We hadn't spoken yesterday evening. We tried, I think. I know I did. But I was too upset to say anything. Too emotional. I'd spent weeks bottling up my feelings, trying not to rock the boat – then when I thought dad was faking it, it was like opening up a can of fizzy drink that someone had been shaking up for a fortnight.

'Yes.'

'Don't worry, Mandy love – it's serious, but I didn't lie: I'm not about to peg it.'

'Neil thinks you might.'

'I might. We all <u>might</u>. You should know that, look at poor Butch.'

'This has got nothing to do with Butch.'

'I've talked to the doctors. I'm not in a good way, and I'm not just going to get better – but there are things they can do. I can get new lungs, a transplant. I'm on a list.'

'But if they can do that, then why not do it now?'

'There's a waiting list. If I could scav a pair of lungs from somewhere, I would do, you know that.'

My dad used to be a strong person. I remember him playing out in the garden with the family. But now he looks so weak – he couldn't pick up a ball without getting out of breath, let alone kick one.

'I would never try to trick you about me dying,' Dad said. 'That would be a terrible thing. If I did do that, you'd be absolutely right to leave the house and never come back.'

I hugged him.

'Been there, done that,' I said. 'Paddy's mum,' I explained.

Dad laughed. 'Oh yes, I remember that. Good on you girl. A girl after my own heart.'

'As long as I'm not a girl after your own lungs, hey?' I said without thinking.

It was one of those things you say on the spur of the moment, that you instantly regret. I went as red as a beetroot.

Dad looked stunned for a moment.

Then his face cracked open into a huge smile and he gave a great roaring laugh.

'That's my girl,' he said.

Neil turned up, and managed to look sympathetic, rather than patronizing.

'Are you OK this morning?' he asked.

'What do you think?'

'Are you and Caleb talking?'

'We are now.'

Neil nodded, looking pleased. 'I'll go up and look after him. Don't worry, Mandy, he's a tough old bird.'

I grabbed his arm. He gave me a funny look.

'What is it that you're planning to do?'

Neil looked puzzled. 'The same as always.'

'Plump up his pillows, open his window so he gets some fresh air? Make sure his oxygen's set up right and that he's taken his pills?'

'That's right,' he said. He still couldn't see where I was heading.

'Then what? That will make him better, will it?'

Neil scowled. 'It will make him comfortable.'

'Comfortable. But not better.'

'He'll be better off than if I didn't do it, yes.'

I spelt it out for him. 'But adjusting a few pillows isn't going to cure his emphysema, is it?'

Paddy had sent me some leaflets and photocopied articles that he'd found, and he'd asked Richie to look on the Internet for him. It was more serious than I realized. The tubes and sacs inside Dad's lungs weren't just blocked up, like I'd thought at first, they'd been damaged, pretty much beyond repair. The lungs are really delicate, all those tubes and sacs are almost microscopic. Doctors can give someone with emphysema some pills with long names that make them sound like dinosaurs – bronchodilators and corticosteroids. They can help maximize the areas of the lungs that work, but they don't really repair the damage that's done.

I explained that to Neil.

'I know that,' Neil replied.

'Then opening a window isn't going to cure it, is it?'

'It will make breathing a bit easier for him. That's what the oxygen therapy is for, too.'

'But it won't cure him.'

'No. I told you: I'm not a doctor.'

'He should see one.'

'He has seen one. More than one.'

'Then what are you doing here? It's a complete waste of time.'

'Caleb needs help.'

'He's got his daughter to help.'

He paused, and looked me in the eye. 'Then perhaps it's you that needs the help.'

I hesitated. There was something about the way he said it. Not patronizing. It was as if he was treating me like an adult for the first time since he'd met me.

'It's difficult coping,' Neil said. 'You're doing your best, but you aren't trained. I may not be a doctor, but I've been on all sorts of courses. I can help, I'm here, and you don't have to pay for me – you might as well take advantage of that.'

'You're worth the money, I'll give you that,' I laughed.

His mouth twitched – he wasn't sure whether I was joking or not. I decided not to tell him, and let him work it out for himself.

What do I think? I think it's good Neil comes around. As I said, it does lighten the load. It hasn't escaped my notice that the other Southampton Dingles have disappeared like dew in the morning now I'm around. Frampton and Key have gone on holiday to Margate (which, apparently, is just like Southampton, so I don't know why they bothered). Job's been round once or twice, but only to sift through his car parts. The others . . . well, these days, I'm not sure who the others are, let alone where they are. A couple of the Southampton Dingles, Bob and Mantha have gone to live with Shadrach, I know that. It's Dingle musical chairs – they've gone up to Shadrach's place because Cain's moved over to Emmerdale. But no one's moved to Southampton to replace Bob and Mantha. They're either too scared of Dad, or too lazy to want to help him.

But Neil's here. When it comes down to it, he keeps coming here. Perhaps he should be an honorary Dingle.

Paddy phoned this evening, and asked if there was any sign yet of when I'd be coming back.

I've still not mentioned Neil to him. . .and I couldn't give Paddy an answer. I told him how serious it was – I lied and said a specialist had come round to the house, and it had been this specialist who told me that there was a risk that Dad would die if he didn't get a transplant. Paddy was almost as upset as I had been – he asked if he could tell Zak and Lisa. I wasn't sure: Dad's known for a while, but he's not told them. He must have his reasons. Even if it's just pride, or he doesn't want to seem weak, then it's Dad's decision whether to tell anyone. So I swore Paddy to secrecy, and he promised that his lips were sealed.

After that, Paddy knew better than to press me for when I'd be back in Emmerdale.

Wednesday 9 August

Neil and I spoke over lunch. Dad was asleep. He's still got a nice smile, but I'd never noticed his hands before. He's got big hands. I don't think what they say about men with big hands is true (and more to the point, Kelly Glover told me once when we'd had a few drinks at the Woolpack, she doesn't either and she's got to be close to being a world authority). But I like big hands. Paddy's got big hands. We just chatted, like real people, for the first time.

He started it, with: 'So where's Emmerdale? I keep

hearing the name. I know it's Yorkshire, but beyond that . . .'

'It's in the Yorkshire Dales. Ever heard of Skipdale?'

He shook his head.

'Connelton?'

'Hotten?'

He hadn't even heard of Hotten.

'Leeds?' I suggested.

'I've heard of Leeds,' he told me, in a tone of voice that suggested everyone knew about Leeds. 'Royal Armouries. Leeds United. Harry Kewell.'

'It's fifty or sixty miles away from Leeds.'

'Is it a big place?'

'No. There's only about two hundred people live there.'

'I get it: sleepy village, no excitement, nothing ever happens.' He laughed.

'Give you a clue: it used to be called Beckindale.'

He looked at me, unsure what to say.

There are some places that will always be associated with disaster. Aberfan. Hungerford. Dunblane. Lockerbie. Towns that had been just names on a map until one day, when, without any warning, something so terrible had happened that no one who ever heard about it would ever forget about them, and the name of the town became the name of the disaster.

On the night of 30 December 1993, an airliner fell out of the sky and onto Beckindale. To this day, no one's quite sure why. They thought it was terrorism at first, in the end I think they blamed some problem with a fuel line. It broke up ten thousand feet over the village, and then the whole area was showered with . . . well, everything: chunks of metal, burning fuel, bits of wings and tail, glass and plastic, engine casings the size of a bus, dead bodies . . . and flowers. The hold was full of flowers, and they rained down for half an hour after the explosion.

Neil sat back, remembering the news reports, remembering the images that the whole country can, if they put their mind to it.

'Were you there that night?'

'No. Uncle Zak was, although he kept his head down. The Dingle place isn't in the village itself, it overlooks it. It wasn't hit. That was the odd thing – you were either hit or you weren't. Only about twenty people died – on the ground, I mean. Everyone in the plane did, of course. And if you weren't hit, you were fine. There were fires, and people buried in the rubble, and dead bodies everywhere – but no real danger if you weren't caught by the wreckage.'

'In such a tiny village . . . it must have been devastating. God, everyone there must still be scarred by that.'

'That's the odd thing: the whole village came together. They knew it . . . well, that it was <u>random</u>, that there had been no purpose to it. The village wasn't singled out, or targeted, or anything. It was just really bad luck. There was nothing anyone could have done to stop it – the chances of it happening in the first place were so small, so it's not like it's ever going to happen again.'

'And so you changed the name of the village?'

'Yeah. A fresh start. You know how it is – still say the name "Beckindale" and people think "crash site". So the villagers voted to change it. It's not like "Emmerdale" is a household name, is it?'

'Like they did with Sellafield?'

He went on to explain that Sellafield had once been called Windscale, but they changed it so that people wouldn't associate it with death and disaster.

I'd already told him it was just like that – perhaps he hadn't been listening.

'So I bet people talk about it all the time,' he said, a little eagerly.

'No. They put it behind them. Whenever anyone talks about it, they call it "the accident". Life goes on. There's a little memorial, and at the end of every year some TV crew turns up to film an anniversary of the disaster story, but that's about it.'

Neil looked at me with a new respect. Which was stupid – I hadn't even been there.

It didn't stop him arguing with me again about Dad's treatment. I think there are more things that could be done. He's ill, and so he should be bumped up the waiting list. If a lung transplant will cure him, then give him a lung transplant – is that really more expensive than paying for full time care? Neil told me it wasn't as simple as that – he says the hospital have thought about all these things. The place on the waiting list takes everything into account: they have to wait for lung donors, then decide who would benefit most from the treatment.

'But this is my dad,' I reminded him.

'There are lots of people's dads on the list,' he said, in exactly the way a primary school teacher would speak to some particularly backward child.

'And how many of them are like my dad?'

Neil looked at me. 'How do you mean?'

'If he was rich, he'd be all right, wouldn't he? It's 'cos he lives in a council house, and he's on benefits.'

Neil shook his head. 'I didn't make the decision, I don't make Health Authority policy – but I really, really, doubt it. Transplants are a big deal – major surgery. And Caleb's been very ill. They might not think he'll make it if he had an operation.'

'Don't say that,' I warned him.

He backed off a little.

'I phoned the hospital,' Neil told me. 'I told them the situation, and I pushed for them to do some more tests.'

'And?'

'And they've agreed. Caleb's booked in for tomorrow.'

'So soon?'

'He was due for one in a couple of weeks, they just brought it forward.'

'So someone else's dad has to wait a couple of weeks,' I said sadly.

Neil nodded.

Neil's a human being, Dad's finally being honest with me, and when the doctors take a look at him, they are bound to sort him out.

Things are moving on.

Friday 11 August

What a difference a day makes.

Dad had a hospital appointment this afternoon. They sent an ambulance round – one of those things they call an ambulance, anyway. It was a minibus, really. I was looking forward to a free afternoon, one without my dad, and especially one without Neil, and a chance to go shopping, or just to do a bit of exploring. So once we'd helped Dad aboard the bus and waved him goodbye, the last thing I wanted to hear was:

'We need to talk, Mandy.'

'We don't,' I told him. 'Let's just keep out of each other's way.'

He smiled at me.

'You're so patronizing,' I informed him.

'We need to clear the air,' he insisted. 'Look – we can't go on like this. I know you Dingles like an argument, but I've seen your dad – he can say the most horrible things, but the next day it's all forgotten. It's different for you. There are things you want to get off your chest. Well, let's talk them through.'

I looked at him. He seemed genuine enough.

'How?' I asked, not having a clue how we could. I wasn't even sure I wanted to. Really I just wanted him to go away. But I knew that wasn't going to happen – the social services would always send someone round. I don't know how it works. But they wouldn't just abandon Dad. If I kicked up too much of a fuss, then perhaps they'd stick Dad in hospital, or a home, or something like that. 'Sit around the kitchen until we work things out? I had better plans for the day.'

'We need to get out the house,' Neil said. 'Spend the afternoon together.'

He smiled at me again. I could tell he meant well.

'You've got the afternoon off,' I told him. 'You don't get many afternoons off. So why don't you just enjoy yourself.'

'Because tomorrow we'll be back to normal and at each other's throats again,' he said. 'But if we have a change of scene, and we just talk about stuff, without the pressure—'

I looked at him. It was a sensible suggestion, I could see that much. It was worth a try.

So I looked at my watch. I didn't need to – the ambulance had come round at twelve, and that had only been a few minutes ago. They had to get Dad to hospital, they always ran a bit late and they had quite a lot of tests to run. They'd drop him off again at about five.

'Two hours,' I told Neil.

'Done!' he said cheerfully. 'Where shall we go? It's a lovely day.'

'It's your stomping ground, not mine,' I reminded him.

Neil said he didn't do much stomping, and asked if I was hungry – because if I was, he knew a really good fish and chip place near the Common.

I wasn't sure at first if he was just doing that 'She's from oop North' thing. Southerners, on the whole, have only the vaguest idea of anything north of Birmingham. It's all flat caps and Man United, with various bits of Hovis adverts and *When the Boat Comes In* put in the mix. Ask them where Leeds goes on the map, and they'll slap it just about anywhere. But they're all confident enough in their knowledge to insist that we keep whippets and ferrets and eat nothing but fish and chips with mushy peas. So I was a bit suspicious but as soon as we went in, the manager came right over. 'Hello, Neil,' he said. 'Who's this, then?'

So Neil was a regular.

Being married to Paddy, and with my own history in the catering trade, I know a good restaurant when I see one. This was an odd one – a bit too posh to be a fish and chip place, a bit too common to be anything else. Formica tables, but ships' wheels and rope on the walls. Every table had little toys and games on it – something to keep the kids quiet. Our table had one of those magnetic fishing games. The place looked a bit old-fashioned, but decent enough. Which was pretty much what I thought of Neil, too.

We sat by the window. There was a good view of the harbour.

'Not used to the water?' he asked me. I realized I'd been staring, and paying more attention to the magnetic fish than to Neil.

'Emmerdale's about as far from the sea as you can get in this country,' I told him. 'We're not that far from Scarborough. An hour? Hour and a half.'

'And Whitby,' Neil said. 'I used to have a cousin in Whitby, and we went up there a couple of times. I remember having a lot of fun.'

'So what's your idea of fun, then?' I said, trying to get into the spirit of things. 'What did you used to get up to in Whitby?'

Neil laughed. 'I was eight. Eight or nine. The same sort of things don't really appeal now.'

'You'll have to get used to them if you've got kids.'

Neil gave one of those grudging laughs. 'Oh, don't worry: I know a Charmander is the evolved form of the Charizard and has a firebreath attack. Or is it the other way round? I'm halfway to being a Pokémon master, I think. You've not got kids, have you?'

'I'm only twenty-three.'

He gave me a look. 'I thought you were a bit older than that.'

That's pretty high up on the list of things a girl doesn't want to hear. 'I'm mature for my age,' I told him, playing with the fish puzzle. 'But no, I don't have kids.'

The manager came out with two big plates of fish and chips. Really big portions.

I started fiddling around with the sachets of vinegar.

'Do you want them?' Neil asked.

I thought he meant the vinegar at first, but he meant 'Did I want kids?'.

'We Dingles like big families. I'm sure I'll have them – but not for years and years, yet. You must have been dead young when you had yours.'

'We were. Young to get divorced, too.'

I'd assumed his wife had died. I don't know why.

'But she got custody?' I said, through a mouthful of haddock. I knew a bit about custody battles – there have been a few in the village over the years. The one thing I knew was that the courts almost always favoured the mother over the father.

'She did, even though she didn't really want them,' he said. The way he said it was – what's the word? – <u>neutral</u>. Like he didn't want to give his feelings away. But it was obvious just how bitter he still was. 'I wanted them, but she got them.'

Anyone with a bit of tact would have left it there. But people with tact always miss out on life, I think. They hear everything second-hand, they're always so busy keeping their head down and trying to be nice that they never amount to much. People who've had problems don't want people to blush and make their apologies and never make eye contact – they want someone to talk to, they don't want <u>politeness</u>, well most of them don't, anyway. So I asked Neil:

'Why did you split up?'

By the look on his face, he was shocked I'd asked at first. His friends – if he's got any friends (and I'm not sure he has) clearly hadn't asked. With Neil, I got the feeling that he'd never really talked to anyone about it.

'She didn't think I amounted to much,' he said. 'She thought I could be more than just a carer.'

I very carefully didn't say anything.

'But it's my life,' Neil continued. 'I think she'd prefer I worked in an office, pushing papers and emails around. But what would that achieve?'

'I've never seen the point of it,' I agreed. 'Filing stuff away and answering the phone all day. You're not making anything, or fixing anything, you're not selling anything, you don't even get to be outdoors.'

Neil grinned. 'She did that. She worked in one of those call centres. Double-glazing. But she didn't even sell it – she just passed on notes to the salesmen and phoned up to arrange appointments.'

'So, what, she found a nice double-glazing salesman instead?'

Neil sighed. 'She didn't even do that. She just left. She said I could have the house. She took a suitcase full of clothes, the sofa, the kettle, some CDs and the kids.'

'Best rid of her,' I told him.

He looked wistful.

'No, you are,' I insisted.

We'd almost finished our lunch. It really was good stuff – fresh catch, I suppose.

'I'll buy you an ice-cream,' Neil offered.

I never say no to free ice-cream. I mean – who does?

We found an ice-cream stand, then sat on a bench and chuckled at each other while we raced to eat the cornets before they melted. Neil started it. He just pointed at my hand and grunted, just as the first trickle of ice-cream managed to seep between my fingers. But, of course, the same thing was happening to his ice-cream. So I grunted back. Then we laughed.

The first time we'd laughed together, I think. We had mouths full of ice-cream, so we couldn't argue. By the end, we were almost on the floor, giggling like we were five years old.

Then there was a moment of silence.

'You've got a nice laugh,' Neil said.

We went for a walk on the Common. I don't know if he'd done it deliberately, but he was wearing a really good pair of jeans. Cut to suit him. OK, OK – what I'm getting at is that I could see he had a nice bum. I wasn't looking, and he wasn't waving it about, or anything, but I just happened to notice.

It was a nice day. A little hotter than I like, but I was seeing Southampton at its best. Neil was keen to point out the sights. A bit patronizing, really – I got the sense that he was reciting stuff he'd learned for his kids' benefit. But I didn't mind too much. We went to the Wildlife Centre that took up one corner of the park and looked at the wildlife.

And he's just a nice bloke, who enjoys walks in the parks and talking about his kids. He obviously didn't want to say anything else about his ex-wife (I don't even know her name), but he's so proud of Ally now she's started school. We went home and sat down at the kitchen table and made ourselves nice cups of tea. And it was like being in a different house – it really was like someone had been in and cleaned up and opened all the windows and filled the house with light and fresh air.

And I've realized something. Neil's stopped saying 'Isn't that right?' I've not said anything, either to him or to Dad. He's just stopped doing it. I think he's starting to respect me – see me as someone who could help him, not as part of the problem. And I think it's the same with me – I see him as a potential partner. Someone who can help me look after Dad.

Talking of which, when Dad arrived back he seemed quite lively. He went into great detail about all the tests they'd run on him. They'd made him blow into some sort of tube (a spirometer, Neil reckons). They did a chest X-ray, and they took a blood sample. 'They didn't give me any results, like,' Dad said. 'They have to examine all the information.

They said they'll write me a letter next week – so it looks like I'll last at least that long, eh?'

Both Neil and I smiled at that one.

'You two seem to be getting on better,' Dad noted.

'We are,' we both said at the same time, then laughed.

'You're a married woman, Amanda Rose,' Dad warned, chuckling.

'We're not getting on that well,' I told him.

But we did have a nice day out, and we have got to know each other better. When I woke up this morning, I couldn't stand the sight of Neil, but now I think it's fair to say that we're friends. Not best friends, or anything silly like that, but we can at least stay in the same room without trying to strangle each other. As I say, you can never be too happy or have too many friends – but I've improved my score on both of those today, and that's got to be a good thing.

Monday 14 August

Same old routine today, but everything felt different. I didn't know the reason at first. Boy, do I know the reason now. But I'll get to that soon.

Neil arrived, and it was like some advert off the telly – all smiles and how-d'you-dos and sunshine and all that. You know them household loan adverts – they start off with a couple looking all miserable, and it's raining and the dog shakes water over them . . . then they take out a bank loan and then you see the next day and it's the middle of summer and the couple look happy, and the dog does something dead adorable. It was like that. For the last month it's been 'before', today, for the first time, it was 'after'.

Even Dad was in a good mood – still basking from all the attention he got yesterday. I can't believe someone got so excited about having a bunch of medical tests done on him, but it's all part of being the centre of attention.

'I was just thinking "This is three doctors and three nurses, all just for me",' he explained. 'I tried to work out what they earned, and I was adding it all up, and thinking I was getting this real bargain.' He spent the morning happy, just reading the newspaper in the garden all morning. I'm not quite sure where he got the newspaper, mind. I suspect the woman from next door will come round later asking if we've had our paper delivered, because her *Daily Mail*'s not turned up.

I tried not to think of all the people who those doctors weren't treating because they were fussing round my dad. I told Neil what I was thinking a few hours later, over lunch. 'My dad is ill,' I said, 'he does deserve the best treatment. As it was, until I made a fuss, the authorities just brushed Dad under the carpet.'

'You might well be right,' Neil said. 'People sometimes slip through the net. That's how Caleb's spent his career, isn't it? Trying to avoid the authorities, not bothering them and hoping they don't bother him.'

'It's like most things in life, if you don't stand up and be counted then you don't get what you want. You have to take risks, you have to speak up.'

Neil looked at me. 'You're so right,' he said, in a really serious voice.

I looked at him. 'Have you got something you want to get off your chest?' I asked. I laughed at the thought of that. It was like Jerry Springer – I half-expected him to say 'Mandy, you know me as Neil, but I used to be Nell', something like that. In the event, what he said came from even further out of the blue than that. Right out the back of the blue. So far from the back of the blue it was practically out of the indigo.

'I think I'm falling in love with you,' Neil said.

I reminded him that I was happily married.

Very quickly he was waving his hands at me. 'I don't mean that I . . . I don't want to cause any trouble. You're fun to be with. Attractive. All I meant was that Paddy's very lucky.' He was about to get up.

'Hold your horses,' I said. 'Where's this come from?'

Neil faltered. 'You haven't noticed . . . I . . . I shouldn't have mentioned it. Forget I said it.'

As you do.

So, of course, I forgot all about it, erased the memory and never let it bother me again. The end.

Or not. I've thought about nothing else since he said it. This afternoon was OK, as it turned out. Dad was no trouble, so I went out into the garden with him. Neil decided it was time to do the laundry and took a couple of big bags to the laundrette. I tried chatting to Dad, but you can probably guess what I had on my mind.

So what do I make of 'the Neil situation'? Why did he do that? Why say what he said? Neil is not an impulsive man. He wouldn't have cleared his throat and said what he did without thinking about it first. I can almost see him practising what he was going to say in the mirror, changing the words, trying out tones of voice until he sounded casual enough. He was waiting for the right moment to tell me, it wasn't something that had only just occurred to him.

For how long?

I've just got no idea about that. I've checked back through my diary, trying to find any hint of it and I can't see a single sign. So he fancies me and he's been sending out the vibes? Since when? The moment he set eyes on me? And what did he expect me to say? 'Fine, I'll move in tomorrow – I just need to phone Paddy first to tell him'?

It's like finding out Graham Clark was a murderer or Barbara the Bag was faking her illness – it's just this moment where everything you think you know about a person just turns round a hundred and eighty degrees. Neil's gone from being this bloke who comes around to help my dad and who loves his kids into this . . . lad who's been secretly lusting after me.

This is my secret diary. So what do I think? What are my innermost thoughts as a man professes his secret burning love for me? I'm not sure I've got any thoughts. If someone came up to me and said 'Write us an opera, Mand, I need it for Thursday,' I'd have no thoughts. Where do you start? I'm sure Beethoven or Andrew Lloyd Webber and all them other opera people would know. But I'd be at a loss. To be honest, if you want an opera written, I'm not your woman.

And it's like that with Neil's 'love' for me. I just don't know where to start. I needed a bit of advance warning of the question. It's sort of flattering, I suppose. At least he doesn't think I'm minging, or anything like that. So what do I think of him?

Well, I know already – I'm warming to him. I quite like him now, and I think he's good and kind. He's not magically transformed into Brad Pitt, though – he's still not much to look at. And I'm a married woman, and I love my husband, even though he snores.

OK. Let's not worry about Paddy for the moment. If Paddy wasn't around – and he is, obviously, but just saying he wasn't – would I go for Neil? No. I go to clubs. I don't still listen to bands that played Live Aid. I don't want kids of my own, let alone some other woman's who I've never met. He's nice. But I don't just want nice, I want a proper man. Neil's got vegetable magnetism, not the animal kind. He's quite nice, but he's not exactly sex on legs.

So, no. Nothing's going to happen.

When Neil got back from the laundry, he was all smiles, and it really was like he'd forgotten the conversation. And the odd thing was that because he was blanking it so well, I started to. We started laughing and joking and all that, and I had to keep stopping myself to think 'Hang on, this bloke said he fancied you'.

I think that's it, end of story. I wasn't even sure I should write it down, because I don't think it's going anywhere.

Tuesday 15 August

I'm on the coach back to Hotten. I've just had a terrible shock.

Paddy's been injured.

Adam phoned, and told me. Then I had to phone Zoe to hear it from someone else, then I called Zak and Lisa to get some words of encouragement. Everyone's being a bit vague about the details, but from what I can piece together, he was up at the stud. I know from his phone calls that Paddy didn't want Adam muscling in on that business. It's a vet thing. Having your hand up a racehorse's bum is more prestigious than having one up a cow's – odd,

I know, but after three years with Paddy, I could tell you the exact pecking order if you wanted. It's all about who your customers are, if you're a vet. The bigger and more expensive the animal is, the more the other vets look up to you.

So Paddy didn't want Adam to be the one who looked after the stud farm. Because then word would spread, and any time anyone who hunts foxes and strangles vowels and doesn't have to work for a living had problems with their horses, they'd call Adam, not Paddy. And Adam would be invited to all the Hunt Balls and garden parties and charity functions, and Paddy would just have to hear about them. Never mind the fact that we both hate going to that sort of thing. We were at a party Lady Tara held a couple of months back, and we both spent all evening saying how uncomfortable we were and how much we hated it.

Although he won't admit it, Paddy's really doing it to get back at Adam – now, that's what I call a proper reason for doing anything. I keep telling him he doesn't need to make any excuses – if he just went around saying 'I want to rub that smug expression off Adam Forrester's stupid face' then everyone would understand.

So Paddy was up at the stud, when one of those posh racehorses reared up and whacked him one with its hoof. They've got strength, horses. Obviously, when you think about it – a racehorse's legs are bred for running. All muscle and sinew and power – and all of it aimed at Paddy's head. People have died like that.

As it is, Paddy's alive. He'll live, but he's unconscious – or at least he was when I got on the coach. I've been out of touch since then, and I've been fearing the worst. I don't have a mobile, there's no time to jump out and ring Emmerdale for an update when the coach stops anywhere. So I've no idea what's happened in the last few hours.

I know the drill from when it happened to Butch, and from Kathy Glover, when she was run over a couple of years ago. The longer you stay unconscious, the more chance there is that you'll get brain damage. Paddy's been out for a few hours, and there was no sign he was responding to treatment. They expect he'll wake up tonight, but they don't really know whether he will or what state he'll be in when he does.

But that wasn't the terrible shock.

I dreamt about Neil last night. That sounds so rubbish, doesn't it? But I did. I probably don't need to spell out what sort of dream it was – put it this way: when I woke up, I thought differently about Neil.

It was the middle of the night, and I lay there thinking about him. Sometimes when I lie awake at night, little problems seem really big, and the big ones just dissolve away, and anything can seem possible or impossible. I thought about Neil and I could see it working.

That was the dream – I was living with him and his

kids in this house. My dad's house. My dad, I think, was still in the garden reading next door's paper. And we lived like happy families. Only I couldn't remember his kids' names. That didn't seem to bother them, though, to be honest. It was all very cosy. We'd done up the house, someone had cleared away all the car parts and scrubbed all the nicotine off the walls. And every evening we went to a night-club or a cinema or a restaurant. A leaflet would come through the door and Neil would go 'Let's go there' and we did, and neither of us seemed to go to work, but we had loads of money. And I cooked them all Dingle Stew and raised the kids properly. No one ever mentioned Emmerdale, and I wasn't even slightly homesick.

And we were lovers. Oh boy, were we lovers.

Reading that back, it's not like I have to write in to Miriam Stoppard or anything to work out what it means. I don't need to draw up a horoscope. Pretty obvious stuff – everything I'm anxious about turns out well. Dad's alive and well in the garden, I'm not homesick, I'm continuing the Dingle dynasty and don't have money worries, and Neil saying he loves me is a good thing, not a problem.

I suspect it's not going to be that easy.

And if things turn out like that . . . it all seemed so rosy and lovely lying in bed last night, but, no, that's my worst nightmare. Why wasn't I still working for Radio Hotten? Why didn't any of my friends from Emmerdale ever call? What happened to Paddy?

And me bringing up a couple of kids like a character from some 50s sitcom? That's not me.

It was so weird. It felt so <u>right</u>, and it's changed my mind about Neil. Made me see him differently. Not as someone I <u>want</u> to go out with, but as someone I <u>might</u>.

I'm worried now – I've just had a thought. What if this is my psychic power coming back? What if this is a prediction of things to come, as it were? Where was Paddy? Dead, after a terrible accident?

But that wasn't the terrible shock, either.

You know when you see *Kilroy*, and it's one that's going on about adultery, like they have every week, and some sad bloke's on there, saying he was happily married and loved his wife, but he was away from home one night and he met a girl and 'it just happened'? And you think 'How can it just happen, you scumbag? How can you <u>just</u> start kissing some bint you met in the bar, and make your wife cry like that? "It just happened", what sort of stupid excuse is that?'

Well, me kissing Neil just happened.

We were in the kitchen. Dad was upstairs – having one of his 'not really getting out of bed' days. And we were making tea for the three of us – macaroni cheese. Yum yum. And I was stirring the pan, and Neil just brushed past me to get the plates out of the cupboard. My bare arm against his hand.

And it just happened.

It was the first time we'd touched. The first physi-

cal contact I'd had for ages. Well, of the nice kind –
I'd had weeks of helping my dad up and around. It
was almost certainly the same for Neil. It's been
three years since his divorce. I seriously doubt he's
touched a woman since – or for a while before that,
by the sound of it.

His hand stayed there for just a second too long. I
looked down at him and he looked up at me, and he
stood up and didn't take his eyes off me.

And it just happened.

I kissed Neil.

We were kissing. I don't remember the middle bit.
I don't remember being 'about to kiss' or 'wondering
whether he was going to try kissing me', or 'deciding
to take the initiative'. So I've no idea who started it.
Neil's quite a good kisser. Eager, not very subtle. I've
never exactly been subtle, myself, though. Tongues
were deployed, on both sides. He kept his hands to
himself, though.

I didn't.

After . . . well, I don't know how long, do I? It's not
like I was timing it . . . we broke away. Neil looked
very serious. I thought he was about to remind me
(and himself) that I was a married woman. 'The
macaroni will burn,' he said.

We kissed again. I was wondering what would
happen next. Actually, no, I wasn't wondering that at
all. I was wondering <u>where</u> it would happen next.
Half of me was getting carried away, the other half
of me was trying to calculate exactly how likely it

was that Dad would come downstairs, and whether going up to my room would be a safer bet.

Neil leant over and turned the pan down. Then he put his arms around me. And if Adam hadn't phoned at that precise moment . . .

God, I've only just thought of that. Five or ten minutes later and we wouldn't have been kissing. We wouldn't have been answering the phone, at least I hope we wouldn't. Dad's got one by his bed – he would have answered, then he'd have come hurrying in to tell me the news and he'd have found me and Neil . . .

What have I done?

I keep thinking that Paddy being injured was punishment for me. I know that's mad – I know, really, that it had already happened by the time I kissed Neil. But the phone call coming just as it did – it's like a sign, isn't it?

No. It's crazy. I'm not going to start thinking like that.

What do I do next? I need to get back to Paddy. I need to get back to my real life and my real husband. I've been away from home, and I was lonely, and Neil was lonely, and we weren't thinking about consequences.

~~So it's good that Paddy got inju~~

No, I don't mean that.

There's a silver lining. It's like splashing cold water in my face – it woke me up. I love Paddy, and I'm not going to put that at risk.

Wednesday 16 August

Paddy's still unconscious.

Nurse Fox joked that there should be an Emmerdale ward at Hotten General – there always seems to be someone from the village there. Apparently, Paddy's sleeping normally, now, rather than being unconscious. I don't know how they tell the difference – it's probably what they're doing when they shine lights in his eyes, which they've been doing once an hour. The early indications are hopeful, I've been told, but it's too soon to know whether there's been any lasting damage.

I love Paddy so much. Seeing him here, lying helpless, peaceful, it's really odd. I know people always say this about people, but Paddy's usually so full of life. I've seen him sleep – I've lain awake loads of times, because he snores so loud, looking at his face, and he smiles in his sleep, his face twitches, he rolls around. I asked the nurse about that: if Paddy's sleeping normally, why isn't he snoring? But the nurse just smiled at me, and told me not to worry.

So I'm sitting here at the bedside, with nothing to do but wait, think – and write up my diary, of course. Right now, the last thing I want to do is <u>think</u>.

I love Paddy, but I feel the same for Neil. Not <u>exactly</u> the same. But I've been in love a few times, and you recognize it, don't you? It's something to do with <u>needing</u> to see someone, and wanting to hear their voice. But despite all those love songs and poems and soppy films, I don't think it's something you can put into words. You just know. So I'm here, waiting patiently for Paddy to wake up, but part of me wants to be with Neil, to see what happens next. Not part of me. It's weird. I love Paddy with all my heart . . . but I also want to be with Neil, and there's room in there for him. I'm not sure how that's mathematically possible, but it's what I feel.

It's so stupid – I'm waiting for Paddy to wake up, but part of me is worried that he will, and he'll look over and see what I wrote. When I started to write this diary, I wasn't expecting it to become a signed confession.

I've just re-read the first entry I wrote in this book. This is meant to be the real me, this is meant to be the whole truth. And now that truth might be awkward or embarrassing, or difficult to face. I'm not the sort of person who gives up on something just because it's hard to do. I'm a Dingle, and Dingles keep their word (on the whole). So I'm going to write down the truth and the whole truth.

Well, I'm not sure what the truth is at the moment. Let me think about that one . . .

Adam turned up, and we had one of those 'I know we've had our differences in the past' conversations, then basically called a truce. I told him I felt really guilty. Adam told me that even if I had been in Emmerdale at the time, I wouldn't have followed him up to the stud farm, and even if I had done that, then

I wouldn't have been able to stop the horse from kicking him.

That isn't why I'm feeling guilty, of course.

I told him I was grateful for what he had done. Adam was modest . . . No. That's the wrong word. He was pretending to be modest. Mock-modest. He <u>said</u> it was nothing, and that Paddy would have done the same for him. But what he was thinking, and what he wanted me to think was 'Look at me, I'm the big hero – I risked my life to save your husband'. That message wasn't lost on Nurse Fox. She pretty much swooned around him, 'Oh, tell me more, Mr Forrester,' 'Can I call you Adam?', 'What shall I make you for breakfast tomorrow morning Mr Forrester?'. I'm immune to his charms – I don't know what women see in him. It really baffles me. He's so full of himself.

So what do I see in Neil?

OK, that's a tricky one. OK, back to the start: do I see anything in Neil? He's not exactly a looker. Paddy's better looking. And Paddy's got a better job. And Paddy isn't pining for his first wife, and doesn't have a ready-made family. And he lives in a big cottage in the Dales, not some bedsit in Southampton.

Why did I do it?

I'm not sure there's a reason. Yesterday I said 'it just happened'. But there's got to be more to it than that. I mean, otherwise, why hasn't it 'just happened' before with a man? I didn't just give Adam a tongue sandwich when he was here. Close proximity? Working together? Not once, when I had my clothes shop over Pollard's barn did I think 'Wonder if Eric fancies a snog?'. Urgh, just the opposite.

So is Neil my 'type'?

Dave Glover, he was my type. He was a good-looking lad – hunky, like one of them doctors from *ER*. He fancied me, too. He married Kathy, and he had that thing going on with Kim Tate, so he never quite got round to me, but he was gagging for it. You could tell by his eyes. Every time I was in the room, you could almost feel it – 'You next, Mandy, just a bit busy at the moment'. Our relationship . . . it was special. I love Paddy, I really love Paddy, but Dave was different – the sort of love you read about in magazines or see on the telly. Our families were at war, he was promised to another . . . it started out like Romeo and Juliet, but it ended in tragedy.

Dave died in a fire, saving his baby son. If you're going to go, I can't think of a better way, can you? Out with a bang, not a whimper. But it never 'just happened' even with Dave. And Neil doesn't even vaguely remind me of Dave. The real love of my life, though, is Paddy, of course. Paddy has his moments. He snores, he used to be a mummy's boy, but he's so romantic. He brings me roses, takes me out for meals, we even went to Venice on our honeymoon. And he's funny. I know this sounds like something straight out of *Woman's Own*, but he's my best mate as well as my husband. He really knows me, better than anyone.

Or did know me.

Part of me keeps thinking 'You know, if I just talked it through with Paddy, we'd soon figure out what I really think about Neil'. Then the rest of me jumps in and goes 'No, shut up, shut up – listen to what you're saying'. I've got to keep this in perspective. I just kissed someone. Got a bit carried away. Then I had a mucky dream about him. But that didn't really happen. I'm not having an affair, I've not done anything too serious.

Yet.

I keep wondering what would have happened if the phone hadn't rung. I think that's just easier to get my head round than trying to work out what I really feel about Neil. Feelings are difficult to describe, aren't they – they don't follow logic. Things just happen. But <u>nothing's</u> happened.

So what would I have done? I think I'd have stopped before things got . . . I don't have to spell it out, do I? We had a snog. Big deal. If the phone hadn't rung, we'd have stopped anyway. We didn't mean anything by it.

Honest.

I'll work it out for myself. Then I'll work out what I do next.

There's a terrible row going on about Paddy's injury. Lady Tara's to blame, according to Zoe – if she had been running the place properly it wouldn't have happened. Sean Reynolds is angry for some reason, I think Ollie was working there or something and he thinks what happened to Paddy could have happened to her. Zoe didn't seem sure what that's got to do with anything.

Zoe's worried about Paddy. She's a good mate to Paddy, and she helped me get back together with him last year, when we thought it was all over. She's worried that the vets practice will suffer, too. Apparently, though, all Tara's interested in is the reputation of her stud farm. Zoe might be exaggerating, or be a bit biased, but I can see that. Tara's not like normal people. Zoe sometimes looks down on ordinary people (even though she likes me, I think, there's always the sense that Paddy could do better, or that I could dress more smartly, or that my tastes aren't very tasteful), and Zoe talks posh. But Tara is from another planet – a planet where polo's something you play, not something you eat, and you don't worry if you lose a £1,000 earring down the back of the sofa, and where a cigarette lighter is a flunky who follows you around and lights your cigarettes whenever you want them to. In her world, 'people' are people like her – people where daddy sits in the House of Lords. Tara was at Edward and Sophie's wedding, you know, not that she ever mentions it. Everyone else is just one of the subjects, even people like Paddy, whose mum lives in a big house in Harrogate. When it comes down to it, Tara thinks ordinary people are there to serve food and make sure the horses are OK, and if a few of them get trampled or evicted, then it's a shame, but what can you do?

AFTERNOON

Paddy woke up.

His eyes opened, and it was such a relief that I can't describe it.

But even then, even as I could feel my heart rising, even as I was laughing and crying at the same time, overwhelmingly happy, a tiny part of me was pointing out that if one out of Paddy or Neil just went away, then that would actually be dead handy – it would sort out my choice for me, and I wouldn't have to think about it again.

Paddy's not lost his memory, as far as I can tell. He can even remember the horse rearing up and the hoof heading towards him. He can't remember the moment of impact – but right up to then, he's crystal clear. He didn't remember Adam rescuing him, of course, and he's really annoyed about that. We both agree on that one – of all the people that could have saved him, of all the people you want to bask in glory, and have people buying pints for in the Woolie . . . the last person you'd pick would be Adam.

Paddy, because he's nice, really meant it when he thanked Adam, and even says he feels a bit guilty about being so nasty to him. He said I looked guilty, too. If he was looking carefully when he said that, he probably saw that I looked <u>panicked</u>, at that moment. I told him that perhaps we should be grateful Adam did what he did.

I think I might have overdone it. I feel so guilty I wasn't here when Paddy was injured, and I kept telling him that. I said it so many times Paddy ended up apologizing to me. He told me how he knew that looking after my dad was important, and he said he felt really bad about trying to stop me from going to Southampton. In fact, he turned around and said, flat out, that if I wanted to go back to look after Caleb straight away, then he wouldn't mind. Paddy said that he wasn't in any danger – but Caleb was obviously gravely ill.

So would I like to go back to Southampton?

That wasn't the question I was asking myself, of course. I'd just assumed I was going to be in Emmerdale for at least a while, nursing Paddy. So I hadn't wondered when I'd be seeing Neil again. I thought I was safe. Could I face Neil? Did I want to face Neil now, or did I want to think about it a bit more, then go back? I was surprised how quickly I decided. I want to stay in Emmerdale for a while, get my head straight. I do love Paddy, after all, I do want to be with him.

'I'll stay here,' I told Paddy. His face lit up – it was obviously the answer he wanted to hear. 'Will your dad be able to cope?'

'He'll be fine, he's got ––––– ' and then I stopped myself. I was a second away from saying it. 'He's got a carer already. Yes, that's right, he's had one for months, and so I've not really had to be down there at all. Yes, he's called Neil. He's really nice. I didn't like him at first, but actually, when Adam phoned we were just snogging, and to be honest we were on the verge of ––––– '. Why not blab it all, Mandy?

But I managed to stop myself.

'He's got that Dingle fighting spirit,' I finished, rather weakly. Paddy didn't seem to notice how awkward I was, he just seemed delighted that I'd chosen to stay. 'Soon as I'm out of hospital, we'll make up for lost time,' he said.

Nurse Fox tells us that they need to keep Paddy in overnight, and they'll want to run some tests, but that Paddy might be home tomorrow afternoon.

I feel so rotten. I feel like such a liar. Poor Paddy. He loves me so much, and he doesn't suspect a thing. I know I've not done anything, not really. But I would have. I know I would have, and I wouldn't fool anyone if I claim different.

I went up to the Dingle farm for dinner and realized that I'd forgotten Sam's birthday. Zak told me not to worry – he understood I had a lot on my mind at the moment. Sam looked disappointed, though. I'm forgetting family birthdays over one stupid kiss that was an accident. I have to pull myself together.

Thursday 17 August

Adam caught me phoning Neil.

I phoned Dad's place to say that Paddy was awake and on the mend. I hoped Neil would answer – I knew he would, really, Dad's too lazy. A quick call, just to give them the news headlines. But the conversation didn't stop there. Neil asked when I was coming back, and, without thinking, I said that I couldn't wait to see him again. He sounded surprised. We got talking. I told him that I'd been thinking about him. Neil says he's been thinking about nothing else. I started to tell him not to be silly, that I didn't mean that . . . but, of course, that's not true.

So I told him that.

After that . . . I can't remember what we said. Well – I can, but I can't remember the words. I get the feeling that if I wrote them down, they would sound tacky, or weird or something. I know this is my secret diary, and I'm meant to put down my thoughts, but I've been trying to find the right words to use. I don't know how to describe it – I suppose we 'talked dirty', but it didn't feel dirty at all. It felt romantic.

Even saying that, it sounds embarrassing, or imma-
ture, or just unpleasant. But it wasn't at all. I felt . . . well,
good. It made me feel sexy. It was like he was in the
room, and doing the things he said he wanted to do.

I'm not helping my case, am I? I'll try to write it
down. I started by saying I'd been thinking of him.

'I've been thinking about you, too,' Neil said. And
it was pretty obvious they weren't pure thoughts.

'Yeah? What have you been thinking?' Teasing
him, letting him know I knew the answer already.

'About how I'm missing you. How I want to see you
again.' Sincere this time, almost deadly serious.

'I want to see you.' I said that quite lightly – I didn't
want it to get too serious.

'Have you been missing me?'

'I have. I've almost forgotten what you look like. I
don't have a photo of you.'

'I've got one of you,' he told me, 'I borrowed it from
Caleb.'

'Did you now? Does Dad know?'

Neil laughed. 'That's right, I told him I wanted it to
put under my pillow.'

I wasn't sure if he was being serious about where
he kept the photo – or whether I thought that was
creepy or flattering.

'Did you tell him what you thought about his
daughter?'

'Oh yes, I told him to make sure it was a photo of
you in a low-cut blouse. I told him I wanted to take a
good look at your chest.'

I'd never noticed Neil doing that. Other men – well, you come to expect it when you've got cleavage. It fascinates them, it's like hypnotism. Busty barmaid, that was me, and I'm sure the pumps in pubs are designed so women have to bend down and the punters get a good look. With me, they get their money's worth.

'Chest?' I asked. A rather prim word, I thought.

'Breasts,' said Neil, like he'd just discovered the rudest word in the world.

'And you just want to look?' I teased.

'Well, it's only a photo, what else could I do?'

'But if I was there, you'd just be trying to look down my top?'

'No. I'd want to touch them.'

'Touch?'

'Kiss them.'

I was getting a bit embarrassed – I'm just as embarrassed writing it down. But the tone of voice . . . Neil was being sincere and flattering and eager, and he was also laughing at himself – playing along.

'You'd let me, wouldn't you?' But it wasn't a question, not really. Neil knew the answer.

And he went on like that, he didn't stop at the 'chest'. He wanted to kiss my face, work his way down my arms, stroke the back of my neck, run his hands down my back . . .

As he carried on working his way south, I realized I had my hand on the back of my neck, and I was brushing it with my finger. I don't remember putting it there, it was like Neil was guiding it. Good job I noticed and stopped myself, because if it had been where Neil suggested . . .

Adam came in as I was talking. He didn't hear me – Neil was speaking. But my expression couldn't have been the sort of thing he'd expect a daughter listening to her Dad to have on her face. Not unless I was telling him the plot of *When Harry Met Sally*.

I think I got away with it. I hung up, very quickly – with a 'Bye, Dad!'.

Adam looked at me for a moment, but didn't say anything. He's full of himself and thinks he's funny – so if he did suspect anything, or even if it had crossed his mind, he'd have come up with some wisecrack. But he didn't.

And I feel terrible, now. While I was on the phone – no, I was really into it. It was odd, it was like we went further than just kissing, even though we were hundreds of miles apart. This sounds so sus, doesn't it? Like I made some obscene phone call, or that the language we used turned the telephone lines blue from here to Hampshire. But, trust me, it wasn't like you could draw detailed diagrams or anything if you had been eavesdropping. It really wasn't like that. It was the way we said things – the tone of voice, the way we knew that the meaning of what we were saying wasn't the same as the words we were using.

But the point is I'm not married to him, I'm married to Paddy. I'm cheating on Paddy. I've not done anything with Neil – OK, there was that kiss, but we've not done anything serious. But now there's someone else in my life. I feel like I'm having an affair, or I'm going to.

I daren't ring Neil back. I told him the news, I can't think of anything else to say. So I know where the conversation's going to go. I need things to cool down a bit before I do that.

OK, change the subject, what else happened today?

Emily came to visit Paddy. I was there, of course. Emily seemed so happy that Paddy was all right. She got all emotional, and explained that when Butch came to hospital, they thought he was going to be all right, but he ended up dying. Paddy's done just the opposite. I got a bit embarrassed, to be honest – Butch was my cousin, and I mourned him, but you have to move on. Emily's dwelling on the death, seeing reminders of it everywhere, and she wants things to be back the way they were. Well, it isn't going to happen. Butch is gone. Emily's talking about spending the rest of her life as Butch's widow. OK, so perhaps she shouldn't be dancing around looking for notches on her bedpost for a decent interval, but to sit there at twenty-whatever-she-is and decide that's it for the rest of her life. . .

I felt like saying 'Look, Emily, Butch was my ex-husband, too', but I do have at least some tact. Emily went on and on – in that meek little way of hers – about how she was glad the Dingles have finally had some luck, and how Paddy was so lucky to have me.

I looked at the bandage on Paddy's head, and tried to imagine the wound underneath it – what sort of mark does a horse's hoof leave? A great big hole, I'd have thought, a deep, wide cut. Perhaps there will be some permanent scar? Well, sorry, Emily, if that's good luck me and Paddy can do without it. Plus, of course, Paddy's not lucky to have me. Paddy doesn't know the half of it. Paddy doesn't know that the moment I left the hospital I was on the phone to another man, saying things I'm not entirely sure even Paddy's ever heard me say.

I bought Adam a pint for saving Paddy's life. The whole pub was full of his fan club – Tara and Tricia were there, acting like the front row of a Tom Jones concert. I'm sure they would have thrown their knickers at him, if either of them were the sort of girl to wear them in the first place. Everyone there was congratulating him, they were almost queuing up to do it. The typical conversation went: 'Adam you're great, Adam let me buy you a pint, Adam you're the hero of the hour, Adam you're so marvellous. Oh, and Mandy, how's thingy? You know that bloke you're married to, who works with good old Adam here'.

Then me and Superman went to Hotten General to bring Paddy home. Adam spent the car journey saying how much he loved Emmerdale, and he could really see himself spending the rest of his life living here, and even when he moved on to bigger and better things he was planning to at least keep a cottage here for weekends. Then he asked if I knew anything about Tara – before correcting himself: I'm dead common, so how would I know anything about the likes of her?

Tara can keep Adam, if that's really what she wants. Adam may be Mr Popular, and have everyone, male or female, eating out of his hand, but he's not worth half of what Neil's worth. Neil works hard, he's interested in his customers and their animals, not his reputation.

I've just written 'Neil' instead of 'Paddy'.

My God.

I meant Paddy.

I mean, what I was saying works for Neil, too. Someone like Neil, caring for old people, sacrificing his own life for a pittance, to make things easy for people less fortunate than himself. Compare that with Adam, who is trying to make a name for himself and for everyone to think he's Top Vet. If Adam and Neil met up – please God, no, don't let that happen! – what would they say to each other? It's like they're the complete opposite of each other. Adam's meant to be good-looking, and Neil's no oil painting. But I know who I find more attractive – Neil's a good person, a genuine person. Adam isn't.

Perhaps that's what attracts me to him – he's not selfish, he's not playing stupid rat race games like Adam does. Neil wants to be happy, he doesn't want vast amounts of money, or status. And that means he's worth ten Adams.

Paddy joined the Adam Fan Club when we arrived at the hospital. But he had to join the queue – the nurses said they were going to miss Paddy, but only because Adam wouldn't be coming around any more. They said that – can you imagine it? Paddy said he could get tired of Mr Perfect. I thought he meant it, but no – he was only joking.

We talked about it when we got home and were safely tucked up in bed – Paddy said he couldn't stand Adam at first, but he's warmed to him, now. I couldn't believe what I was hearing: I felt betrayed. Paddy laughed. 'You always bear grudges. At first, yes, I looked at him and thought he was a smoothy with a naff haircut, and everything was just an act, but he wasn't very good at it. But then Adam saved my life. That's going to change my opinion of him.'

'He's milking it. He was in the right place at the right time.'

Paddy looked at me. 'You sound like you wish he wasn't.'

'I'm glad someone saved your life, but why did it have to be him?'

Paddy grinned. 'I know what you mean. It would have been nice if someone else had done it. Someone I like. But it was Adam. And he did risk his life – there was nothing to stop the horse lashing out at him, too.'

Paddy's right, of course, and he's right that I bear grudges.

Though he's been allowed home, there are some things he's not quite up to yet – and having that great big bandage on his head isn't exactly a top turn-on. So when he went to bed, I told him I was going for a shower, then came down here to write up my diary. That's something I hadn't really thought about, to be honest – it's not like I can do what I was doing before, and write my diary in bed, last thing at night. Shame, I'd got into the habit. I'm also going to have to think hard about where I hide the diary. Paddy doesn't snoop around my things – but he might find it accidentally. For now, I'll hide it in my suitcase, in the little compartment Uncle Zak sewed in. But I may have to look for a better solution. I don't think I'll be able to write up my diary every day while I'm here. I'll do my best.

Tuesday 22 August

Kelly Glover used to be my best friend. We had fun together, shared secrets, told each other things we'd never tell anyone else. Emmerdale's a small village, and there aren't many people our age. Well, Kelly's younger than me, but only by a few years and she always was what charitable people call 'old for her age'. But sometimes friends drift apart as they grow up.

Kelly's always had a colourful life. Both her parents are dead now – her mum a long time ago, but her dad was killed on Christmas Day. That seems to be when things started going wrong for her. I . . . I'm not going to go on about it. I was there for Kelly, but she wouldn't listen. She suddenly became obsessed with marrying Roy Glover. No one really understood it at the time. I didn't. I like Roy, but . . . well, Kelly's in a different league, and she'd always known it. She had Chris Tate panting after her for a while.

I think Kathy is the great love of Chris's life – actually, I know it. You can see it in Chris's eyes whenever Kathy's going out with anyone else. I don't know Chris Tate that well, I don't want to know him. Perhaps he loves Kathy so much because he sees her as his conscience, someone that brings out the best in him. He needs it. Normally he's . . . not <u>evil</u>, that's such a big word, such a strange one to use about someone you know. It makes him sound like something out of *Austin Powers*. But Chris is not nice, he gets what he wants and doesn't mind who he hurts. And that's why he needed Kelly. A not so innocent young girl, one he could buy off and lavish affection on, and who would let him do what he wanted, and would never tell him he was doing anything wrong. The exact opposite of Kathy, in fact.

Perhaps I'm just used to thinking like this because of all the horoscopes I do, or all the magazines I read. But Chris is an intelligent man, he must have thought about it. Kathy's his sugar, Kelly's his spice. Kelly lived at Home Farm with Chris for a while. She was mixing it with Kim Tate and Zoe and that lot. So why settle for Roy? I like Roy. He's honest, he works hard, he's loyal. And he's never going to be anything. Like a lot of village lads, his ambitions don't even stretch as far as over the next hill. He might 'make it as a DJ', but all that'll mean is he buys a van and drives around Skipdale and Connelton – maybe even as far as Hotten for a special occasion. Kelly's ambitions . . . I'm not entirely sure there were any limits to them, to be honest – she wanted someone with a yacht and a sports car. Roy Glover can't even spell yacht.

Once Kelly was my friend, but not now. She changed when she married Roy – she stopped listening to people. I know your dad dying is going to affect you – but she's not the only person who's lost a parent. It wasn't really like that with Kelly, anyway. It was like the <u>real</u> Kelly had turned up, the grown-up one, who realized that you didn't always get what you want, and that life isn't always fair. I know why she changed. But I can't bring myself to write it down. This diary is about my secrets (and there are plenty of those, now), not about Kelly's.

How can I put it? Her brother – her stepbrother – Scott came back from a stint in the army, and he was a changed man, and Kelly liked the changes. I think what happened after that is best described as a dishonourable discharge. Even a year ago, I'd have been dead sad to see Kelly go, but she's burnt her bridges with me. She wouldn't listen to her friends as she went into . . . well, it got rough for her. But even when she tried to kill herself just after Christmas, I only thought 'You stupid girl'. She didn't want to die, not really. If it was a cry for attention, or an attempt to draw a line or whatever, it didn't solve anything.

But now Kelly wants to get away from her past, she wants to make a clean break. Kelly and Roy are leaving the village. They're off to Ibiza, to live with Roy's dad, Ned. Ned in Ibiza! That idea still makes me laugh. Ned was a hill farmer, a good bloke, like Roy, and like Roy he was planning to die where he was born – in Emmerdale. He had it rough, too – a son dying, a wife going loopy. But he got out. He met a childhood sweetheart, Dawn, who was off to Ibiza to open a bar. And, all credit to him, he realized that this was his chance to be happy, and he followed her there. I can't picture it myself – Ned Glover Goes Large In Ibiza. I'm sure stranger things have happened, but you'll have to give me a while to try and think exactly what they might have been.

Ned turns up from time to time – all suntanned and smiling. Quite a different person to the one we knew. Roy and Kelly know they've got to do something, that they have to get out, and so they're catching a plane to Ibiza to start a new life. They think that all they need is some Balearic sunshine and then they'll be smiling, too.

Kelly came over tonight, and I thought at first that

she was trying to sort things out between us before she left. That may have been her plan, but that's not how it worked out. She kept going on about how wonderful Ibiza is going to be, and how she's going to have a tan the whole time, and how she's finally getting what she wants – married to an Ibiza DJ, and living in the hottest resort in the world, surrounded by all the rich and famous. Well, I told her a few home truths. I told her that I felt sorry for Roy – he's a good lad, and deserves better. I reminded her exactly why she was leaving. She's not leaving in triumph, she's running away, because she's got nothing left here. This wasn't Roy finally hitting the big time – this was Kelly dragging him down into the gutter to keep her company. Even now, whenever she opens her mouth it's all about what she wants, what her new life is going to be like, how she's come out on top. She barely mentioned Roy. It could be a chance for her to change. Start again.

I know what it's like to have a reputation – it's impossible to shake off. Years later, people remember something you did. People never remember the good things about other people – only the mistakes. Say something nice to someone, and they'll feel good for a day or two – say something nasty or critical and they'll never forget it. Kelly didn't say many nice things to people, and there aren't many people she's kept on side. What can I say, in Ibiza her 'lifestyle' might go down a bit better than in a small Yorkshire village. It might really be a chance to get away from Viv and Scott and memories of her dad.

When I moved to Emmerdale, my slate was wiped clean. It was like I'd just come into the world – little mistakes and indiscretions, a couple of the dodgier boyfriends and murky bits of past, and things I did when I was a teenager and didn't know any better . . . well, no one cares any more. It happens. When people go to university, or move to the city, or start a new job in a different part of the country they get a chance to start again. You only take those bits of the past that you want to. You can reinvent yourself. You make new friends, go to new places, find new things to do.

So this is another chance for Kelly. It's the perfect opportunity. Ned doesn't really like Kelly – in his speech at the wedding he said pretty much everything he could without using the expression 'village bicycle' – but he loves his son, and because of that, he respects Roy's decision to stick with Kelly and try to make it work.

And Ned's with Dawn, his first love. A woman who, as far as I know, has managed to live with Ned for a whole year without kidnapping a single baby, or doing any of the loopy things Jan, his first wife, did. And their bar's doing really well. When Lisa and Roy worked together, he kept telling her how proud he was that Ned could do what he did, make such a big leap and make such a success of it.

So the Glovers could be exactly the sort of happy family that Kelly's never had but she's always wanted. They won't be worried about money, they won't have to save up to go on holiday, not unless they get sick of sunshine and the best clubs in the world. This could be exactly what Kelly thinks it is – the fairytale ending.

But it's not, is it? We all know it's going to end in disaster.

I hope she and Roy find happiness there. But I don't see it happening. I told Bernice later that I'm glad Kelly's going. And I meant it. I give them just long enough for Kelly to realize that however good the weather is, Roy Glover is still Roy Glover, and he's still got a crap haircut. Roy's more patient, quieter – but at about the same time, he'll realize that letting Kelly loose on an island full of randy men with their own hotel rooms is not the recipe for a happy marriage. Let's see – it's Tuesday now . . . I give them until the end of the week. Call it Friday.

It reminds me, of course, of my situation. Sort of. It makes me think. What's the future going to hold? The horoscopes aren't much help at all. I've tried drawing one up, but there's just nothing there I can use – it's stuff about facing a choice and being at a crucial point in my career. I know that already, I don't need Jupiter and Saturn to tell me that. I want to stay with Paddy. I love him. He's my husband – I wouldn't have married him if I didn't want to spend the rest of my life with him. And Dingles don't go in for planning careers – Dingles don't go in for <u>careers</u>, full stop.

Bernice used to have a Plan, a book where she

had it all mapped out for her, with little lists to tick things off. Find Mr Right, marry Mr Right, have two kids, a boy and a girl, she'd even named them. It really was at that level of detail and every single aspect of her life got a page, all in that very neat handwriting of hers. When she first came to the village, she was working for a temp agency and looking for her ideal man – a year on, she was land-lady of the Woolpack and was engaged to Gavin, who met all her exacting criteria.

Hurrah for planning?

Hardly. There were some things about Gavin that weren't on Bernice's list – like the fact he tried to shag any woman that came into his sights . . . and that he didn't always confine his romantic activities to women. I think it's fair to say that catching Gavin in a compromising situation with Paddy's cousin didn't figure in Bernice's Plan. She's abandoned her Plan, now, realized that life throws these things at us, that someone isn't working out what we do months in advance – or if they are, they're keeping schtum about what they've got planned for us.

If there was a Mandy Plan somewhere, then Neil wouldn't figure on it at all.

I wasn't planning to kiss Neil. I didn't think that afterwards my legs would turn to jelly at the sound of his voice on the phone. That's just not like me at all, and it scares me. I don't think I'm in control of this situation. And as much as I want to write down 'and it won't happen again', I just can't. I've no idea what happens next, or where I'll be in a year's time. With Paddy, <u>probably</u>. But not definitely.

It's . . . I just never thought I'd have these feelings again. I thought I'd find Paddy, and we'd settle down and all that jazz. And I really love Paddy, I do. Seeing him on that hospital bed made me realize how much I'd missed him, how much I'd been taking him for granted.

But if I can feel this way about Neil, then I can feel this way about other people. And if Neil fancies me, then who knows who else there is out there? I thought I'd ticked 'Find Mr Right' on my list, I thought I'd done that.

But now I'm not sure.

Neil's not Mr Right. I don't think he is – I still don't really know that much about him. Was it a very specific set of circumstances? Being away from home, the stress of Dad being ill, being close to Neil all day, every day, being annoyed with Paddy because he was frustrated about my trip to Southampton and wanted me back? Like in a horoscope, where weird things coming together can lead to strange things happening? A conjunction, a set of events that only happens once every thousand years, or whatever?

But what if it's every year? Or every six months? I just don't know. I need to see Neil again to make my decision. It'll be a gut feeling. Obviously, sooner or later, I'll be going back to Southampton, I'll have to see Dad. And Neil will be there, and I'll take one look at him, and I'll know.

I hope.

That's the plan, for the moment, though – I'll let things settle. There's no rush.

Wednesday 23 August

After all that fuss yesterday, Roy went off without Kelly.

I can't help but feel that <u>that's</u> the fairytale ending. Roy gets to escape the clutches of the wicked witch of the Dales, and flies away to the land of sun, sea, sand and DJing opportunities. Of course we're still stuck with Kelly in Emmerdale, but perhaps she'll start to realize how she's ruining her own life and other people's. We can but hope.

It was so funny seeing her trooping into the Woolpack, carrying all her suitcases, looking so miserable. I worked it out first – Roy dumped her at the airport, the veil was finally lifted from his eyes. So I took great enjoyment as I told everyone assembled there exactly what had happened. So much pleasure that Bernice told me to stop. But, no, chances like this come less often than comets – I milked it for all it was worth. I made sure I said what I had to say.

I got a letter from Neil.

Well, <u>Paddy</u> very nearly got it. He's always up

before me, he's always there for the postman, when he comes at about half eight. Except this morning. Because of the accident, he's taking it easy, and I've been making a special effort to get up earlier, to make his coffee and to look after him. To be honest, I'm just getting up the same time I did at Southampton. And caring for Paddy is like being on holiday compared with caring for Dad.

So it was up to me to pick up the post. There wasn't any junk mail, there weren't any bills, just one letter, in a little white envelope with a Southampton postmark on it. I thought at first it was from Dad, and wondered why he hadn't just phoned. Then, without opening it, I realized who it was from. I tucked it away in my diary and put that at the bottom of my bag – I knew already that the letter wasn't the sort of thing I would want to be reading when there was any chance of Paddy coming in. After Adam nearly caught me telecanoodling the other day, I've been paranoid about it.

So I went upstairs with Paddy's coffee, a lovely sweet smile on my face. Paddy was up, and getting dressed. He asked what was in the post.

'Nothing,' I said.

'I heard the letterbox,' Paddy insisted.

'Oh, just some flyer from GK Supermarkets,' I told him. 'This week's special offers. I put it straight in the bin.' Paddy looked a bit disappointed.

'Oh come on,' I told him, 'you didn't really want to read it.'

Paddy thought about it. 'I suppose not.'
But I wanted to read my letter.
Paddy's not recovered enough to be back out on his rounds yet, but he's doing paperwork and other vet stuff down in the surgery. So I've snuck up here and I've just read the letter.

Dear Mandy
I've been thinking about you all the time. I know it must sound silly, I know it puts you in an awkward position. But I think I love you. I think being honest about it is best – I could keep pretending, and being on my best behaviour, but what good would that do?
The first time I saw you, I was bowled over.

The first time he saw me I was in my dressing gown telling him to get lost!

You are beautiful. And you say what you think, you do your own thing. You're a strong person, someone who doesn't let life mess you around. I wish I could be a person like that. I don't think you realize how attractive that makes you. You get what you want, and that's so sexy.
I know you're married, I know you're happy with Paddy. I don't want to embarrass you, or put that at risk, I'm not saying you should leave him, I'm not expecting you to. What I'm saying is

that the kiss was special for me. It meant a lot. I don't know what you thought, I know you didn't plan it, or expect it, and it was probably a mistake. But just being there with you, kissing you, being so intimate, so unexpectedly. . . I've thought about it again and again. You're a great kisser – I don't know how I measure up, I don't know whether I should ask! I want to do it again. I don't want to stop there. I want to get to know you.

You know I've been thinking about you. I was hoping you'd call me, I know I can't call you. And I think we both enjoyed that phone call. When I was waiting for the call, I knew what I wanted to say to you, I planned to say what I said, and talk like that to you. And I meant everything. I want to be with you, I want to say all those things to you in person, I want to touch you. I want to know what you think, I want to know what you feel about me.

I don't want this to sound creepy, and I know it does. It's just that since my divorce I've not so much as looked at another woman. I wasn't on the look out. But you're so special, and I've got to tell you what I think.

You've got a lovely smile. You're beautiful, and—

He goes on to say I've got a sexy body, and he goes on about that for a while. He clearly enjoyed writing that bit – and he's obviously put a lot of thought into it. Which is flattering, I have to admit.

I can't wait for you to come back. Look, don't worry – if you never want to see me again, after all the things I've said, then I would quite understand. If you don't feel the same way, then obviously I'll have to go. Ask for a transfer.

But I had a choice – tell you and risk losing you, or not tell you and have to live a lie, pretend I was just there to look after your dad. I don't know what you think, but I want to know – even if it's to tell me to push off. You're married, I know that. I don't want to split up a marriage (that sounds so arrogant – I know I couldn't possibly do that), but if your feelings for me, if you've got any, if they are anything like mine towards you, then please tell me, I need to know.

I read it and I read it again and rather than read it a third time I was almost going to call a taxi and go straight to Hotten Coach Station to jump on the first coach to Southampton. Instead I took a deep breath and decided to write my diary instead.

I've calmed down a bit now.

I want Neil. I don't just mean ... y'know, that I want him physically. I want to get to know him better, I want to hug him and reassure him, and tell him that I've really got feelings for him, too. I want to find out more about him. I've found out more about Neil in the week we've been apart than in the time we spent every day together. I've thought about him more as a person since I came back.

Does absence make the heart grow fonder?

But . . . being here with Paddy, it's not very <u>exciting</u>. Paddy's spent the day filing vets records, and he wouldn't even let me join in. I didn't have a massive urge to file, you understand, but I've not seen my husband much for a long time, I was keen to be with him.

Paddy nearly died. You'd think that would throw everything into sharp focus – that such a shock would remind me how much I love him, and how lucky we are to be together, and safe, and all that. It did . . . but only a bit, and that's what's surprised me. Paddy's still just Paddy – I'm glad he's alive, obviously, but the shock he nearly died wasn't quite like the splash of cold water I thought it would be. I love him, I realize that I love him more after the accident than before, but not so much that any thought of Neil's gone from my mind.

No, it's obvious what's going on – I've managed to turn Neil into this absurd fantasy figure, and I'm comparing boring old Paddy with that fantasy, not with Neil as he really is, or how he'd really be. So it's not really fair on dear old Pad. I've fallen in love with Imaginary Neil – the one I dreamt about, the one I've built up as this wonderful, caring man. When I was in the room with him I couldn't stand him. Apart from a quick snog, a moment of madness, I was never attracted to him. He loves me, but it never even occurred to me to fancy him. He's just not my type. If I saw Neil in the flesh again . . . as I say, I've been back through my diary, and everything I ever wrote about him was how irritating I thought he was, how much I hated his voice, and how he has annoying little habits. So when I go back to Southampton, I'm going to be confronted with all that, and it's going to hit me just how stupid I've been.

What I have to do is get down to Southampton, shatter all my illusions, then get on with my life. But for the moment, I'm going to spend some more time with my husband, I'm going to live my real life. I'm going to enjoy all those things I missed out on those months in Southampton – I'm going to get back to Radio Hotten, I'm going to have a drink with my mates, I'm going to go to see my family. Reality.

Thursday 31 August

I feel a bit trapped in Emmerdale, now.

Tricia and Marlon held a dinner party for me and Paddy. With Marlon handling the catering, the food was really great, as you'd expect. Trish's attempts at cocktails were a little more . . . interesting. You'd think a barmaid would have got the hang of things like that by now.

Trish and Marlon have just been on holiday together, and they are obviously very much in love. They could barely keep their hands off each other. Trish passed the holiday photos around, but she'd forgotten to check through them first – so all the topless ones were still in there. Paddy, to his credit, was pretty embarrassed and didn't really know where to look (he settled for sneaky peeks when he didn't think I could see him) but Marlon was utterly mortified. Paddy pointed out that we'd not had a holiday for ages – and suggested we went where Tricia and Marlon had gone. I told him I wasn't keen on a beach holiday, and we've left it a bit late this year. He seemed a bit disappointed, but agreed.

To be honest, I don't want to go on holiday with Paddy. It'll . . . this is going to sound really harsh. It would only be me and Paddy, it would just be a bit hotter and we'd be by the seaside. It wouldn't feel <u>special</u>, I don't think.

And I'd be thinking about Neil.

I can't get him out of my mind. I just want to find out about him. I want to talk to him, I want to go places with him, I want . . . OK, I'm going to admit this, now, brace yourself – I've started to wonder what Neil would be like in bed. It's stupid, isn't it? I've started to daydream about it. Not in great detail – I just find myself wondering what it would be like. The thing is, I could find out. I know I could. I was on the verge of it before!

I just feel passionately about Neil – he's a mystery.

Paddy's comfortable, cosy, I already know what he's going to say before he says it. He's predictable. As we were leaving, I just knew the last thing Paddy would say to Marlon was 'That was great, we'll have to do this more often – our place, next time'.

We even talked about this on the way home. Paddy put it best – we've lost our spontaneity. You look at Marlon and Trish, and they're falling in love. They're still learning, having to do new things as they get to know each other. They can still find out stuff about each other. They're starting all those silly things you do when you're falling in love – significant firsts (first holiday, first time you invite your friends round, all that sort of stuff), they're still coming up with silly names for each other. Marlon's still at that acutely possessive stage, where mention of a past indiscretion is crushingly embarrassing.

Paddy said that we are in love already – we've settled down, we're beyond that stage. And it's sad in a way, because we can't really surprise each other. If I'd told Paddy what I was thinking at that moment, I'd have surprised him, I can tell you.

I'm falling in love. I know all that. I know the excitement, I know the thrill. I want to find out everything about my lover, I want to be alone with him. I know exactly how Tricia and Marlon feel, because I feel exactly the same way. I'm falling in love, it's an incredible, liberating experience and I don't think anything else in the world matters. I'm falling in love and my husband knows nothing at all about it.

I've not even spoken to Neil for a week. I've been trying to get him out of my mind. I want to stay here, make it work with Paddy. That's the ideal solution – all that passion and curiosity, but about Paddy. I want to fall in love with Paddy again. I do love him, but it's not the same thing as Tricia and Marlon. But I'm not. There are times where he's boring, to be honest.

I think about Neil the whole time. It's because I can't tell anyone – I'm bottling it up, and I'm sure if I could tell someone, then they'd just say 'That's really stupid, Mandy. Just do this, this and this and then everything will be sorted out'.

Throughout my life, I've not stopped to think, I've got on with it. Things haven't always gone one hundred per cent my way, but looking back, I don't think there's a single thing that I've done that I would change, or anything I regret. No, in an ideal world, I wouldn't have taken that swing at Pollard that ended with me punching out Stella and getting three months inside. And if I'd have kept my gob shut in court, I probably wouldn't have got three months. But what was the alternative? Letting Pollard get away with victimizing me? Letting the magistrate just walk all over me – getting my say in court, letting people hear my side of the story – that's more important to me than just being nice and polite and watching what I say.

Staying in the village, I have to think before I say anything. Anything at all, in case I mention Neil, or his kids, or the fish and chip shop, or the fact that I fancy him rotten. I've nearly said something about him so many times.

This diary's kept me sane and saved my marriage, I'm sure of it. It's the one place I can get it all out into the open. It's like I'm talking to someone, sharing what I think. It doesn't matter that no one will ever read it – God, I hope no one's ever going to read it – it's somewhere where I can say what I like without worrying that anyone's going to find it.

But I do. I worry that Paddy's going to find this book and read it. I keep it in my bag, or hidden right at the back of a drawer in the bedroom behind a load of junk, where I'm sure Paddy's never been.

There is no way I'm going to Southampton like this – I'd do something stupid. I'd elope with Neil, or phone Paddy and tell him it's all over. I know I don't want that really. I've not even been married a year. OK, I lived with Paddy for a while before that, but it's not that long since it was all gondoliers and romance. If I dumped Paddy and ran off with Neil then I know full well that Neil would be just as ordinary, just as predictable before much longer. More. With Neil I've <u>never</u> had the romance, never had that. Why do I think that I would? He couldn't afford to take me to Spain, he would split his time between me and his kids. And while a vet's life is hard, I've seen Neil at the end of a long day, and he's utterly worn out. Paddy's just better on all scores. And I do love Paddy, I do. I hardly ever write it down here because I take it for granted. It's not something I think about – except when something like the accident makes me think about it – it's something I know. So, sit it out, wait until this stupid crush wears off.

I think this is going to be easier said than done.

Friday 1 September

How do other people manage to have affairs? I don't understand how they can cope with it. Look round Emmerdale. I think everyone's had one at one time or another. Off-hand, I can't think of anyone who's been in a relationship for any length of time without straying a little. I don't think Emmerdale's particularly unusual for that.

Emily and Butch. Once again, Emily and Butch show the rest of the village how it's done. Loving each other and only each other. Not fighting, or having illicit romances, or sneaking around with some bedroom secret or another.

But despite that, I have to say I've got a sneaking respect for those people who manage it. How did Gavin jump out of bed with Bernice, nip up to Stella at Home Farm for an afternoon of rumpy, then pop back, kiss Bernice on the cheek and carry on like he'd just been into Hotten to buy a new shirt? How did Sarah Sugden and Richie get away with it for so long – him a lodger at the Sugden's farm, with three kids and a husband who was never more than a couple of hundred yards away? I mean <u>where</u>? <u>When</u>? That was the first thing I wondered when I heard about it. Jack didn't suspect a thing – but they must have been at it upstairs while he was in the kitchen. Where else could they go? Richie's office, with Pollard downstairs and Scott Windsor in the next room? I suppose if they wanted a roll in the hay, then living on a farm must be quite convenient. They must have planned it like a military operation to make sure no one found out. This is a very small village, and we all know a great deal about what everyone gets up to. It's very difficult to keep a secret in a place where everyone knows everyone else.

That's the thing about 'it just happens' – it doesn't, not really: it's like horoscopes – a combination of things all have to happen at exactly the right time. Like when I kissed Neil – if one thing had happened differently, if Dad had been downstairs instead of upstairs, if I'd been making the meal, if I'd got the plates out first, if Adam had phoned a few minutes earlier – nothing would have happened. All these people didn't 'just happen' to have affairs, they had to make an effort. Not just to start the affair in the first place, but to carry on with it without partners, friends or even innocent bystanders spotting anything's up.

It's tricky enough for me at the moment, with Neil in Southampton. Just from reading this diary, it's obvious that he's top of my mind a lot of the time. I feel so guilty. Paddy will say the most innocent things, and I'll go bright red and change the subject. I feel guilty every time I get a phone call, just in case it's Neil. I have to go down first thing and check the post to make sure Paddy doesn't see anything he shouldn't. I've not had any more letters . . . but I've phoned him twice since that phone call. Those conversations were a bit more tame – but we were comfortable with each other. I even said 'Love you' at the end of the last call. I didn't think about it, I just said it, just automatically. Like 'See you soon' or 'How are things?'. I say it to Paddy on the phone, and Dad, and possibly a few other people – Zak and Lisa, perhaps. But it's not a casual thing. I've never accidentally said it to Seth or Roy or anyone like that. Doesn't even occur to me. So why say it to Neil? What could I be trying to tell myself? I'd already hung up before we got the chance to make any more of it. Just imagine if Neil was lodging with me and Paddy, sharing a house, helping out with the break- fast.

Most of the time I cope by just shutting it away – Neil's from another world, there's nothing here to remind me of him, no mutual friends, no chance of him and Paddy becoming best pals, or anything like that. I phone him, he doesn't phone here, in case Paddy picks up the phone.

If Sarah flipping Sugden could cope, then how come I'm in such a mess? How did Sarah manage to organize it? She was working at the Diner at the time, before Kathy sacked her, so she was out all day. Richie spends his day driving around in that sports car drumming up business for his computer company. First thing in the morning, she'd be too busy making packed lunches and making sure Andy, Robert and Victoria are ready for school. When she got back, surely, after she'd cooked everyone's dinner (and I don't imagine for a minute Jack Sugden helps with the washing up) she'd be too knackered to do anything.

I'm half tempted to ask her how she got away with it for so long, or how she found the time, or if she's got any hints, but I think that might be a bit of a giveaway. Perhaps it's precisely because being a working housewife means she's organized and able to break up her life into little compartments – perhaps she's got a little shopping list or one of those wipeable whiteboards up with a list of things to do:

Do shopping (need bread)
Wash Andy's games kit
Make mad passionate love to lodger on kitchen table
Take mince out the freezer
Listen to *Woman's Hour*

I was going to say 'But she'd be stupid to write it down', but that's what I'm doing, isn't it? I'm glad I started this diary, now. I still have the nagging suspicion it's going to be used in court as evidence against me, but it reminds me what I've really been thinking, not just what I remember thinking. This book is keeping me honest.

And there's a moral to the Sarah story – once Sarah was found out, it's all been ruined – Jack's thrown her out, she can barely see the kids, who don't seem to understand what she's done to them. And everyone in the village looks at Sarah like she's the Scarlet Whore of Babylon, or wherever it was the Scarlet Whore came from.

It isn't right to carry on like this. That's my gut instinct. If only it was that simple, though – my instincts are also telling me to go with Neil, and go with Paddy. Not carry on the affair – just pick Neil. And Paddy. I can't have them both, but my instincts seem to be too stupid to work that one out.

Thursday 7 September

I came back home today to find Paddy setting up candles, smoothing out the best table-cloth and carefully selecting some good music and wine. My woman's intuition told me pretty quickly that he had a romantic dinner planned. I panicked for a moment, assuming that there was an anniversary, a birthday or some other special occasion that had slipped my mind. What with one thing and another (OK, OK – what with Neil), I thought I must have forgotten something. As I started thinking, the only thing I could remember was that I'd managed to forget Sam's birthday.

But I worked through all the dates I could think of. It's not my birthday, it's not Paddy's, it's not our wedding anniversary, the anniversary of us getting together, the anniversary of the night we first – ahem – became intimate (we usually celebrate those last two together, anyway), the anniversary of us getting back together after the vet's ball . . . by then I was running out of things. But no, there's nothing at all that I can think of in September. Usually, Paddy's a big kid, he can't keep a secret. If he's got something planned he goes all coy and pretends there's nothing up. But this one caught me out.

'What's the occasion?' I asked.

'Jason said that,' Paddy replied a bit exasperated. 'I just thought it would be nice to have a nice evening in, that's all. It's what young couples do, isn't it? Spontaneity. We said we wanted some. Ta-da!'

Can't fault him on that.

I started wondering what Neil's idea of a romantic meal would be.

But quickly stopped myself.

I enjoyed the meal. Paddy said that it had been a long time since we did anything on the spur of the moment, and I couldn't really argue. What with Paddy's job, having to go and see Dad, Butch dying, and all the other things that have been going on, we've not really had much time to ourselves.

But tonight was romantic. Just the two of us, the phone off the hook, candles. And, on the rare occasions that he bothers Paddy's a good cook.

It was intimate, just the two of us, enjoying each other's company. When we got to bed, it was like old times – passion, excitement. Not the first time since the accident, but the first occasion that we'd made time for each other. But – and this is a terrible thing to admit – I thought about Neil. Not the whole time, nothing like that, but I didn't get carried away with Paddy, there was always a part of me thinking about Southampton and Neil. I don't think Paddy noticed, and I don't think it put a damper on the evening – just the opposite, I think we're getting on better than we have done for months.

I've tried to think back, tried to work out what changed and where we went wrong. It's not been the same since we got married. That sounds really terrible. I don't think that it's <u>because</u> we got married, or anything like that. But when we got back, we moved into Zoe's cottage (because she'd bought Home Farm, so the cottage was rent-free). On the face of it, that was quite a step up from my room at the Dingle farm. This is a proper house. OK, it's got the vet's surgery at one end, but even with that, it's a big place, with a really good view of the village.

But my room was dead cosy, and it was mine, not just somewhere we rented. There wasn't central heating, but there was a great little stove, and we kept ourselves warm. And it was <u>fun</u>. I tried to make

Zoe's place fun, and I've done my best to brighten the place up. But that led to tension, right from the word go. I've not earned much this year – Pollard threw me out of the barn, shutting down my business – and he reported me to Trading Standards. Then, what with prison, Dad and marriage, I wasn't able to find regular work until my radio stuff (and that's not brilliant pay – I mean it's dead easy, I'm not complaining, but it's not like I'm on Chris Evans money). And, due to one thing and another, like the fact I used to be self-employed and I'm not always available for work (because I have to go down to Southampton), and because Paddy earns what he does, I can't really claim much benefit.

That's not a problem – we Dingles aren't afraid of exercising our rights, but we prefer to stand on our own two feet. We don't bother the system, they don't bother us. Well, that's the theory, it's not always how it works out.

So I don't have much money of my own. Paddy's rolling in it. Vets don't earn as much as you'd think – they're not <u>poor</u>, don't get me wrong, and Paddy's definitely earning more now he's a partner, but he's not on Chris Evans money, either.

But he's always been . . . what's that word Emily uses that means thrifty? . . . Frugal, that's it. That means he's stingy, let's be honest. I mean, what else describes someone with thousands of pounds saved up in the bank? Just sitting there, doing nowt? It's not normal, is it? He saves up for things, rather than just buying them on a credit card. He likes to pay cash for things, rather than going for finance. He's always getting junk mail – get our gold card; no get our platinum one; no, over here, take advantage of our introductory rates. I totted them up, one morning, if you added up all the offers, he could have borrowed over a hundred grand. That was just one morning. If I was him, I'd take them all up on it. It seems rude not to.

So when it came to decorating the house, he's the finance, and I was the designer. It was good fun – but it led to arguments about money, and a lot of it became the <u>house</u>, not us. Does that make sense? Instead of it all being about us, and what we would do, and all that, it was suddenly about what colour a wall would be, or where we'd put the sofa.

I was scared when Paddy almost died. I'm so pleased that his recovery has been so fast. The accident did remind me how much I love him again. But I realize now that I love Neil, too.

And it feels wrong, I feel so guilty.

If it felt right to leave my husband and go down to Southampton, I'd do it. It wouldn't be easy – but it would be easier than living like this – saying one thing, meaning another, always watching my words and blushing and looking guilty at the slightest, most innocent thing someone else said.

And I should have learnt by now to be careful what I wish for. I wanted Paddy to be more spontaneous and he managed to be that tonight. Oh yes.

A couple of bombshells.

It started out predictably enough. Paddy talked about a holiday again – but I reminded him that I couldn't, because of Caleb. He realized it's been a long time since I was down there, and suggested he took some time off and we spent a week there – sort of a holiday.

I very quickly persuaded him that looking after Dad isn't what anyone would call a holiday. I said it was a shame, but sooner or later I'd have to go back, and it's best if he stayed in Emmerdale (this, of course, is true).

He said it was a shame, then dropped bombshell number one – he's had an idea: we've got room here for Dad – he should come up to live in Emmerdale. He got quite enthusiastic.

This is bad news. No more Neil, but still having to care for Dad. From Paddy's point of view, it's not perfect, but it's the best compromise. But Paddy doesn't know all the facts, does he?

I brushed him off. Said I'd think about it. (I am thinking – I'm thinking 'No, no, no!'). I told him we'd both have to think it through carefully – it had serious, long-term consequences. Paddy agreed – and said it seemed to be a proper, permanent solution, and much better than me having to uproot myself and spend months at a time away from the village and my life.

And if Neil wasn't part of the equation, he'd be absolutely right.

But bombshell number two was worse . . . Paddy's been rethinking his life following his accident. It really made him think – with people his age, or even younger, like Rachel and Butch dying, he's been thinking that there's no time like the present.

For us to have kids.

I tried very hard not to shout out 'Eh, you what? Where are you getting that from?'

I managed, I think, to look quite enthusiastic. But I told him it was a big decision, and we shouldn't rush into it. He's young, he's healthy (now!), and he's got years left in him yet.

Paddy was disappointed, I could tell. I told him I'd love to have his children, but not just yet. We were going to spend the rest of our lives together.

I almost convinced myself.

Wednesday 13 September

I'm feeling trapped.

I checked my horoscope. Events have been set in motion, and the next two weeks will be a time of great emotional turmoil. I feel like I'm losing control of the situation.

Paddy hasn't forgotten about his idea of bringing Caleb up here.

He laughed about it. 'It's not the ideal solution, but it could be worse.'

'How? ' I asked. <u>If we do that I'll never see Neil again</u>, I thought.

'Well I could be suggesting that my mum comes to live with us.'

I had to laugh. I could see Barbara the Bag coming to live with us, but pigs would have to fly <u>and</u> hell would have to freeze over first.

'My dad can be just as bad as your mum,' I told him. And I wasn't lying. He's a real pain. One of the things that made Southampton bearable was the fact that I knew I could escape. If Dad came to live here, then how could I escape him?

'You make us sound like a pair of primary school kids,' Paddy chuckled. 'But it's logical, isn't it? Unless you're really keen on Southampton.'

Not Southampton – just one of the people who lives there. But, of course, I can't tell Paddy that.

Paddy looked at me that way he does – pleading. I recognize the look. Please be reasonable, Mandy, just think about it.

I hesitated. It just struck me that I couldn't go on like this. I'd known that, of course, I'd known that for weeks, but suddenly I <u>felt</u> it.

'I'll go down to Southampton tomorrow and ask Caleb,' I told Paddy, surprisingly myself with what I was saying. 'I can't guarantee what his answer will be – if he doesn't want to make the move, I can't force him to.'

I realized as I was saying it that this was just the right thing to say. I can go down, see Neil again, help get my thoughts straight. Then, and only then, I'll worry about Dad. Whatever I told Paddy, there's no way at all I'm going to ask Dad to come up here until I'm sure that's the best solution. But if I do choose to stick with Paddy, then I'll want a clean break – to forget about Neil and Southampton.

I could never be just friends with Neil. And that would mean if I told him that, then Dad would have to move up here. Neil could no longer be his carer. Even if the social services did agree to reassign someone to Dad (and from what Neil's saying, Dad was lucky to get someone at all – there aren't exactly people queuing up to do his job), that wouldn't solve the problem. Neil lives down there. I could bump into him shopping at West Quay, or walking on the Common. I could never go for fish and chips at that place we went to, however nice the food was, however much I wanted to hone my toy fishing skills – Neil might be in there. And at any point I was down there looking after Dad, if the doorbell rang it could be Neil. Or, and this is what I'm really scared of, I know, I could just pop across to see him one evening.

In a way, it's good that I'm being forced to make a decision. I knew it would have to happen one day, I was just hoping that the perfect way out would just drop into my lap, or I'd wake up in the morning with a lightbulb over my head, working out the way to get everything I want. I know now that's not going to happen. Paddy seems to have made his mind up – I caught him telling Jason that Dad was moving in, and suggesting that Adam might want a lodger at Mill Cottage. I reassured Jason, and told Paddy to hold his horses – I reminded him that I hadn't so much as mentioned the idea to my dad yet, and it was entirely possible he'd say no.

But Paddy seems to have it all mapped out. This evening we went up to Zak and Lisa's place for dinner. It started off OK – Zak warning Charity about Terry's penchant for younger women, Charity assuring him that it wasn't like that at all, and Terry was just a mate. I wasn't worried about the age difference – but I told Charity that Terry worked for the Tates, and not to forget that they were the people that killed Butch. Everyone else round the table nodded their agreement – family loyalty is the most important thing. We were all Dingles, by blood or marriage, and we stuck together. And everyone was so busy agreeing with me, they didn't see my face as I realized what it was I was saying.

It got worse. After we'd finished eating, we all started cooing round baby Belle. She's two on Christmas Day, and she's growing up so fast. I don't even know if she's a baby any more – she's becoming a toddler. She's adorable, whether she's technically a baby or not. And Paddy just said she might have a playmate soon – there might be the pattering of more tiny Dingle footsteps.

Zak and Lisa assumed I was pregnant – well, after Paddy said that, what were they meant to think? I very quickly set them straight. I was very annoyed with Paddy. But what was I going to say? I was biting my tongue. I was angry, and like I keep saying, I've got a gob on me – I knew that I might just blurt out exactly the wrong thing to say. 'Children? Paddy, I'm not even sure we should be together?'

So while I was carefully not saying anything, Zak and Lisa kept going on about how wonderful it would be to have another Dingle in the world, and how Belle was one of the best things that ever happened to them, and how important it was, and how it was my Dingle duty. And he reminded me that he was one of five, and he'd had five kids, and so had Caleb, and it was a Dingle tradition. I'm sure he's lost count somewhere along the way.

Lisa said she couldn't understand what was stopping us.

'Because I'm not sure I love Paddy, and by tomorrow night I might have left him for someone I met in Southampton.'

I didn't say it. Of course I didn't say it.

But Emmerdale's gone from being paradise, with clean air, family and friends, to a place where I'm constantly being nagged at, where people are making decisions about my life without telling me. And just when I thought it couldn't be any worse, Paddy put his foot in it again.

'Anyway, we might have our hands full soon with Caleb.' I'm pretty sure he was trying to change the subject. From Paddy's point of view, that's exactly what he was doing.

Zak went a bit white. 'Caleb?' He didn't fancy the idea of Caleb up here, breathing down his neck.

Emily wondered if we were moving to Southampton.

'We thought about that,' Paddy said. (When? We didn't discuss that at all. When Paddy was concocting his plan to get Caleb up here, that must have been one of the options he left on the drawing board. How long has he been working on this behind my back?) 'But we decided that we were getting a bit fed up of Mohammed going to the mountain all the time, so we're going to try to get the mountain to come up to Emmerdale.'

'Caleb,' he clarified for Sam's benefit. 'We're going to offer Caleb the spare room at the cottage.'

Zak chortled. 'Make sure you move Jason out, first, eh? I'm not sure Caleb would want to bunk up with anyone, least of all a—'

Jason's moving into Mill Cottage with Adam. Well – as Adam's lodger.'

I held my hands up. 'Hang on a second – this is just one of the things we've talked about. Dad doesn't even know we've talked about it yet.'

Zak thought about it for a moment. 'I've not seen my brother for a long time,' he said. 'It'll be good to have him here, in his hour of need. And it'll be good to have many Dingles in one place.' Then he looked at me, all dewy-eyed. 'And perhaps with another one on the way.' And they all raised their ale cans to toast Paddy for being such a great bloke.

There's far more chance that there's going to be one less Dingle around the place, especially after tonight.

I'm furious with Paddy.

Thursday 14 September

I've made up my mind. I've chosen between Paddy and Neil.

I've chosen Paddy. I'm going to stick with my husband.

OK. You might not see how I got to that decision from where I was last night when I was writing my diary downstairs, furious with Paddy for what he'd said about babies and Caleb and all that. So bear with me.

I went upstairs, I got into bed with Paddy, who had this very contrite wide-eyed look on his face. I told him he could look as hopeful as he wanted, there was absolutely no chance of nooky.

And I didn't sleep last night. I lay in bed, with Paddy asleep next to me and I felt so rotten.

I love him. He started working as a locum for Zoe three years ago. We hit it off dead quickly, we went out a few times, it was something of a whirlwind romance – which is the Mills and Boon way of saying we didn't exactly hang around before we ended up in bed together. Then Paddy's contract was up, and he disappeared off to Cumbria. He came back for me, but then he went off to Ireland.

And I realized just how much I loved him when we were apart. This is beginning to look like a familiar pattern, isn't it? Anyway, I thought he'd gone for good, and Colin Batty showed interest in me. I wouldn't have said no, to be honest (to be <u>very</u> honest, I didn't!) but Paddy returned, he swept me off my feet (which is easier said than done), Colin zoomed off in the sunset on that bike of his, and the rest is history.

I don't know what my life might be with Neil, but I know what I've got with Paddy. I know I love Paddy. With Neil . . . I like him, he's a nice bloke. But I don't think it's love.

Reading back through this diary, it's obvious I've always had strong feelings for Neil – I started off hating him, he made me angry, then irritated the hell out of me, then that became strong sympathy for him, a real appreciation of what he was doing for my dad – then it became attraction and that somehow managed to turn into lust while I wasn't looking.

With Dad being ill, with me being away from home, it meant I was feeling . . . I don't know quite what the phrase is. Highly-strung? Worked up? Emotional, anyway. I've never bottled anything up or had any problem expressing my feelings. But when I'm on my home turf, surrounded by friends and family, I get an outlet for it. I get to vent my emotions. Like with Kelly – I got to tell her exactly what I thought of her, then I got to laugh my head off when it all fell apart for her.

When I am in Southampton, I only see Neil and Dad, give or take the odd newsagent and door-to-door canvasser. Dad's ill, I don't want to cause him any stress. I'm there for him, it's not fair to expect him to bear the brunt of what I'm feeling. Besides, I don't want us to argue, because . . . because he might not be around much longer. There, I've said it. I don't want him to die in the middle of us arguing about something. Or in the middle of the night, after we'd had words the previous evening. I want us to be at peace.

So I can't be anything but the dutiful daughter with Dad around. I fetch things for him, talk to him, listen to all his stories. I keep what I'm feeling bottled up. I don't talk about how I don't want my dad to go away, or how old that makes me feel, or how there are things I want to tell him but I can't. This is not the time to be selfish.

But for the sake of myself, I have to draw a line. I've always been an all or nothing kind of girl. I've always known my own mind. I think that's what's really scared me about all this – a couple of weeks ago, if you'd told be that I'd be even thinking about leaving Paddy for another man, then I'd have laughed at you. This snuck up on me, I've never been in charge of the situation – it's all 'just happened', there have been all sorts of accidents and events beyond my control. I've had this choice hanging over me, but instead of doing what I'd normally do, I've just let it drift, let whatever's happened happen.

This has to end.

I'm not the sort of person that sits down and works things out logically. I go with my gut instincts. Sometimes that gets me into trouble – I say things I regret, I do things on impulse that someone else would have stopped themselves from doing. I've hit a few people. That makes me sound like I'm irre-sponsible, that I'm just not in control of my actions. But of course I am. What I'm trying to say is that I tend to act, rather than think. That doesn't always work out, of course, but I've done all right for myself. Like anyone, I've had points in my life where I've had big decisions, I've had choices to make. But that's never stressed me out at all, because I've always <u>known</u> the answer straight away. And I've done all right for myself. On balance, if I'd been Meek Mandy, sitting in the middle of the classroom, afraid of expressing myself, obsessing about what other people did, and how they looked and what 'proper' people did. Well, what would I be doing right now? Well, Uncle Zak would have been evicted, for one thing – more than once. I'd probably be mopping the floor in some hamburger place, or folding up size 10 tops in a branch of Top Shop, I'd be the one writing to the radio presenter asking for an autograph, rather than the one signing them.

There's that expression about the meek inheriting the earth, or whatever. It's just not true. Emily's meek.

She's not even going to inherit her dad's farm, now. She's hard-working, she's a decent person, she always does what's right. And look at her. Poor Emily.

There's no way I'm going to be Poor Mandy.

Usually I just go with my feelings. But here, my feelings are saying 'have them both', and I know I can't. That's what's confused me.

I've thought about it.

In practical terms, I probably could just about manage to have them both. I already split my time between Emmerdale and Southampton. So why not just have a bloke in both places? Paddy can't come down to Southampton, not with his job, and Neil's not going to turn up one day at Zoe's cottage. So, they're nice and separate. Mandy Dingle, the girl with a man in every port.

But my gut says that's wrong. Of course it is – I feel so guilty already for betraying Paddy, and it would be so unfair on Neil. It wouldn't be fair on either of them. I'm married to Paddy, but he wouldn't know anything about it; Neil would know everything, but he would also know I was committed to Paddy in a way I just couldn't commit to him. However much Neil said he accepted that situation, there's no way he could ever be happy like that.

But now I've chosen.

Paddy.

I'm going to live with Paddy, in Emmerdale, I'm going to get Dad up here, by hook or by crook.

I doubt Dad's thought about moving up here, but (once he's had a good think about it) I suspect he'll go ahead with it. In Emmerdale he can be looked after by the family. It won't just be me, of course, there are plenty of Dingles here to help out. And say what you like about my family, they rally round when there's a crisis, or when one of us needs looking after. Dingles care for their own, and family obligations are more important than anything else.

And it's too late to change my mind, it's already gone beyond the point of no return. I suggested my plan to Paddy. Missing out the real reason I was so keen to draw a line under Southampton, of course. Paddy almost danced around the house singing Hallelujah.

'I've just told you my dad's coming to live with us – I can't believe you're celebrating.'

I wonder if I was <u>hoping</u> Paddy would strop, so I could use it as an excuse to leave him? I doubt it, somehow – that's only just occurred to me. I know my mind works in a strange way, sometimes, but it usually keeps me up-to-date with what it's got planned.

'I'm happy 'cos it looks like there's a weight been lifted off your mind,' he said.

'How do you mean?'

'Well, since you came back, something's obviously been bugging you, hasn't it?'

I said nothing and acted casual.

'And all this time you've been wondering how you

can look after your dad without spending so much time away from home.'

I nodded. This was going really well so far.

'You silly thing. You had me really worried. I thought I'd done something to upset you, or that something had happened in Southampton you hadn't told me about.'

'Like what?' I said, pushing my luck. Had Paddy worked it out?

'You know, like an argument with your dad. Something like that.'

I smiled. 'No.'

'So Caleb's ready to just pack up and live here, is he?'

I hesitated.

'He doesn't actually know,' I admitted.

'Eh?'

'Well, I wanted to make sure it was OK with you before I asked him. I'll go straight away. I said yesterday that I'd go today. Well, no time like the present.'

This was going really well. Very smoothly. It was going to work.

'The 4x4 will be big enough, won't it? If it isn't, Zak will let us borrow the van, even though it's short notice, won't he? I doubt we'll be able to hire one so quickly.'

My expression must have been a dead giveaway, because Paddy said.

'Didn't you think I'd be coming along?'

'I just thought I'd go down on my own,' I said.

'Your dad's not going to be able to pack and move all those boxes, is he?'

'I'll get Job and Frampton to help out.'

'Those two'll just disappear at the first sign of hard work. You'll end up doing it all.'

'But what about work?'

'Slow day today – Zoe and Adam are both around, so they can cover. It's a quiet time of year.'

I was thinking 'Paddy, don't come down – you'll ruin everything. I need to break up with Neil. I can't do that with you there, can I? Don't ruin it all now.'

But I said: 'To be honest, we can come back up on the coach with a couple of suitcases – you know, essential stuff. We'll arrange to pick up the rest later. It's all junk, anyway. Half of it's only in the house because Dad never throws anything away.'

'I don't mind.'

I was trying to think how to get out of this one.

'Pad . . . Dad doesn't know he's moving yet. I need to talk to him. Alone. I have to persuade him. Dad's a stubborn old man, he might take some persuading, and I think it's best just coming from me. If you go down, you could—'

'Cramp your style?'

I laughed, and tried not to sound too nervous. 'That sort of thing.'

Paddy smiled. 'OK, whatever you want. How about I give it a week? I'll hire a van and come down.'

A week. A week to finish with Neil. That will be

fine. It'll take five minutes. Once I've worked up the courage, it'll take five minutes.

'Make it next Sunday – that way you won't need to take time off work,' I said.

Paddy was grinning. 'Phew. I was dreading being there to tell your dad, to be honest.'

I was puzzled. 'I never thought you'd be happy to see me going off to Southampton.'

'Of course – this is the last time you're going there isn't it?'

I must have gone very pale. I just had a terrible twinge – a week from now, and I'd never be seeing Neil again.

But it was only a twinge. I know I've made the right choice. Gut instinct.

'What's up?' Paddy said, seeing me hesitate. 'You hate the place. Never mind – I'll come and rescue you. You go and pack a bag, I'll phone for a taxi.'

And we kissed, and now I know we'll all live happily ever after.

So relief all round. Problem solved, normal service will be restored shortly.

I just thought I'd write up my diary first.

AFTERNOON

OK, I'm still in Emmerdale.

As soon as Paddy went out, I realized I'm just not ready to face Neil.

I was packed and ready to go, and Paddy kissed

me goodbye. But as soon as Paddy was gone, I phoned to cancel my cab. I sat around. I wrote my diary, for heaven's sake. I couldn't stay in the house after that, I just walked around the village, trying to get my head straight.

It's ridiculous.

I've got two things to do in Southampton – 1) tell a man I've had a quick snog with, but know very little about, that I don't want to see him again, pointing out that I'm married and very much in love with my husband. And 2) tell possibly the most cantankerous, awkward and stubborn human being in the whole world that I've decided he's got to move north, without giving him the <u>real</u> reason why he has to.

If Neil wasn't around, I'd be terrified of giving my dad the news. All the Dingles are scared of Dad – Zak respects him, wouldn't dare say anything against him or do anything against his wishes. All the other Dingles are just the same – Ezra and Shadrach treat him like Marlon Brando, and even members of the family who live by their own rules – Cain springs to mind – would do exactly what my dad said they should do.

Dad's not lived in Southampton that long – he only moved the rest of the family down south a few years ago, that was after I'd moved to Emmerdale. No one's quite sure why he upped sticks and left his precious home turf in Crumpsall. At my wedding (which Dad was too sick to attend), I heard Cousin

Jerome mention something he called 'the incident'. But no one else seems to know what it is – Uncle Zak tried to pretend he knew when I asked, and that he'd been sworn to secrecy on pain of summat or other, but it was obvious that he had no idea and was just saying that to make it look big and clever.

But Southampton's where Dad calls home now. And the way he talks about it, you'd think he'd lived there all his life, and the council house he's in has been passed down to him by generations of his Dingle forefathers.

Getting him out of there is not going to be easy.

But I'm not even thinking that far ahead. It's telling Neil I'm dreading.

I'm not worried about Neil's reaction. It's not as though he's going to clout me one, or ring Paddy up and spill the beans, out of pure spite. Neil just isn't like that. He'll take the news calmly, he'll look a bit sad, then he'll say something sweet like 'Oh, I knew it was too good to be true'.

And I'll be the one that gets sad and angry, and I won't be able to tell him how difficult it was to choose without it sounding patronizing and without it changing the fact that he gets nowt for winning the second prize.

I don't doubt my choice, not at all, but I'm going to hurt someone, someone I . . . love. Yes, I think it's safe to say that I love Neil. Not as much as Paddy, let alone enough to leave Paddy for, but in a very short time, Neil's made me question myself, he's surprised me. If Paddy wasn't around, then things might have been different.

I bumped into Jason while I was hanging around the village. We went to the Woolie, and I bought him a pint. I feel sorry for Jason – he's another victim of my problems, being forced out of his home. But he didn't seem to mind – he said it was in a good cause, and I was very noble for doing what I was doing. He saw my rather shamefaced expression, and asked me if there was something on my mind. And I almost told him, there and then in the Woolpack Bar.

I needed someone to talk to, and Jason's a good lad. He kept his own secret for so long, being scared and guilty because he couldn't tell his family that he was gay. And when his family found out, they threw him out of the house. It's not right – and now I'm throwing him out of another house, just to suit my own selfish purpose. And I thought it was only fair to tell him why I was doing it. I trust him, I don't think he would have told Paddy. I geared myself up to tell him everything about Neil – growing close, the kiss, the letter, my doubts. If I had said anything, then Paddy would have heard – he was right behind me.

I covered quite well. Paddy wondered why I wasn't on the coach, and I told him that I felt I had to apologize to Jason for kicking him out. Paddy thought that was really sweet, Jason said there really wasn't any need – he knew how important my dad was to me. Group hugs all round and everyone was happy.

Just a second later and . . . that would have been it. Everything ruined.

And it wasn't over yet. I needed to hear Neil. So I phoned him, and he was so happy to hear my voice, and I could imagine his little face lighting up when I gave him the news that I was on my way back down. Hearing his voice again . . . I admit it gave me a bit of a thrill. It's just knowing how much he likes me, knowing that someone so nice likes me so much.

It got a bit flirty. I wasn't making an obscene phone call, nothing like that, but it was just the way we were saying things. It's difficult to describe – if I just wrote what we said down here, you'd think it was a perfectly ordinary conversation. Neil was at Dad's place, of course, and I think that was enough to stop him getting too carried away. It was just a nice, fun chat.

I told him I would see him very soon.

I didn't want to spoil it by telling Neil that it was over. I didn't even hint. I want it to be fun while it lasts. I've not promised him anything, I'm not going to lie to him, or lead him on – but telling him my decision will be like bursting one of his kid's balloons.

When I was fourteen my first boyfriend dumped me by phoning up and telling me I was dumped. I could never do that to anyone. So I was being very friendly with Neil, enjoying it while it lasts. And then Adam came in. I hung up almost straight away.

'Are you sure that's your dad you were talking to?' Adam said, thinking he was being dead funny.

'We're a very close family,' I reminded him.

'You'll be seeing him every day soon, you'll be sick of the sight of him.'

I was so annoyed with Adam. It was like he was playing gooseberry, or he'd invited himself along to Paddy and me having a candlelit dinner. It was quite good to be annoyed with him for two reasons – he thought he was doing me and my dad down: how dare he sneer at me looking after my dad when I've chosen to nurse him through his illness? And how dare he presume to know who I am, or what I'm thinking? I know what he thinks of me – he treats me like one of those pets he looks after, he thinks I'm good for a few laughs, and that I'm 'fun', and that's all I am.

He saved Paddy's life, but that doesn't mean he can talk down to me.

It's all very well blaming Adam for my problems, but that's not what's happening at all. If I wasn't hiding something in the first place, then it wouldn't matter if Paddy or Adam, or anyone else, overhead what I was saying.

You've probably spotted that I'm spending a lot of time thinking about the Neil situation. Of course I am – I can't get what I have to do out of my head. And it's stupid – I've made my decision and the more I think about it, the more I'm sure that I've made absolutely the right choice.

It was nice hearing Neil's voice. I fancy him, of course I do. If I was single, I'd be down there right now giving him the time of his life. This hasn't been an easy choice.

But I'm not single, and I have made my choice.

If I stay here, then it's not solving the problem. I'll get caught. Twice today, so how many times tomorrow? I have to be caught out <u>once</u>, that's all. Once. Just one slip of the tongue, one time where my diary falls out of my bag and someone finds it, one morning where Paddy sees the postman before I do, or Lisa phones up Caleb and it turns out I've not been phoning him half as often as Paddy thinks. God – the phone bill is itemized! Have I ever rung Neil at home? I've got the number, but . . . no, I don't have it. I could always pretend it's the social services.

This is mad.

I know what I have to do. I'm not going to change my mind. The longer I stay, the longer I put my marriage at risk. I have to get this over with.

EVENING

Right. I'm on the coach.

Plenty more faffing about since this afternoon, when I wrote all that stuff up there.

Up to Zak and Lisa's place, to 'say goodbye'. Quite rightly, Zak pointed out that I don't usually go to all that trouble when I'm off to Southampton. He guessed that I didn't want to bite the bullet and talk to Dad.

'You'll never persuade Caleb to do anything he doesn't want to do.'

That hadn't even occurred to me. What happens if Dad just puts his foot down and says 'no'? Well, I tell Neil anyway, that's what. It'll be tough, but I think I'll even manage if Neil stays on as Dad's carer. I can work alongside him. I'll draw the line, agree to be friends – and I'll understand if Neil never wants to see me again.

Lisa gave me some advice. 'Don't let Caleb bully you, just tell him straight.'

You could see the fear in Zak's and Cain's eyes – they wouldn't dare stand up to Dad, they wouldn't tell him anything. They'd ask. They'd suggest. And Dad would just ignore them and do what he wanted.

Then I went home and waited, still not wanting to go.

Paddy came back – he couldn't believe I was still there, and wondered what the matter was. He fussed around, tried to hurry me away. He joked that he wasn't trying to get me out the house for any reason – it wasn't like he had a fancy woman on the way round or anything. I forced myself to laugh. And again when Jason promised to keep Paddy on the straight and narrow.

'This is the last time,' Paddy said. And he's right. That's the best way to look at it – the last time I spend the best part of a day on a packed coach, the last time I leave my husband, the last time I have to put myself through all this.

This isn't going to be easy, but it's not easy living a lie in Emmerdale.

Sunday 24 September

I've not written my diary for over a week. Because there's been nothing to report.

I've been hinting to Dad about moving to Emmerdale, but I've not come out and suggested it yet. I've just been saying how great it is there. I'd got some photos with me, and I made sure Dad happened to see some of the more sunny and pleasant looking ones.

He's got Neil to move him downstairs – there's a bed made up in the front room now. Neil's convinced it's for the best: Dad can now go out into the garden without going up and down the stairs, he can make his own meals. It's meant to make him more self-sufficient, but I can't help but notice that Neil seems to be doing more than ever for Dad.

A couple of days ago, Dad said Emmerdale looked very nice, that he hadn't realized how big our cottage was.

'When you said cottage, I thought you meant a poky, draughty place,' he said.

'No, it's dead big,' I told him. 'Loads of room.'

He looked at me, and I thought he was going to invite himself up. But he didn't.

If I can get him to think it's his idea, that's going to be the battle won. That's always the best way to get your way with someone – convince them that it was their idea in the first place, and they are <u>so</u> clever for thinking it up. Paddy falls for that one every time. So I'm hoping I can keep dropping these subtle clues, and eventually Dad will go 'I've just had a marvellous idea'. Perhaps it's wishful thinking, but I reckon the thought he could be a freeloader in the Dales has occurred to Dad already, and the crafty old git is trying to work out how he can con his way into getting me to agree.

I know I'm right: he was reading the paper this morning, and there was this shock exposé about the state of rural policing. He read it three times, and kept reading out some of the quotes – 'scarcely any police cover', 'response time of up to three hours', 'one policeman for every four or five villages'. There was a glint in his eye, and I could tell what he was thinking – this sounded like Dingle Paradise to him. I very carefully didn't mention that Zak and Lisa lived next door to a policewoman.

And he gave me this funny look. I played it cool. 'Oh yes, Zak loves it, you can get up to all sorts of mischief.'

I was very careful to say 'you'. 'You can get into all sorts of mischief'. I'm playing it subtle, trying to get him to put the pieces together.

Dad seems to be better than he was – following those tests he had, the doctors changed his medicine, and it's obviously had an effect. It's not a cure, or a miracle, or anything like that, but he just doesn't seem as lethargic as he was before – he's got more energy. He still gets out of breath – but now he can work up the effort to get out of breath, when before he just couldn't be bothered getting up.

I reckon it was a problem with his old pills, rather than any property of the new ones. I've read about that happening – you take something to cure a stomach ache, and it gives you depression, or you take a painkiller because you've got a sore leg and the next thing you know you're shoplifting and you can't remember how you got there. So my dad's problem might be his lungs, but the tablets he used to be on could have sapped his energy.

But he's much better now. I'm almost looking forward to him living with us. Before I was dreading it – it was only something I accepted because it was worse than the alternative. But now I can really imagine him in Emmerdale, enjoying a drink at the Woolie, sitting on a bench with Seth, trying to get Sam to help him go poaching at Home Farm. He's a city Dingle, I doubt he's ever poached an egg, but he'll really get into all these countryside pursuits, I can tell. I know what he's like, he'll be trying to work out how to apply his urban cunning on us stupid locals.

He's going to come a cropper – we're not as daft as all that in the country. Seth Armstrong's as cunning as a fox.

I haven't mentioned Neil yet.

I'm here in Southampton to finish with Neil. I esti-
mated that it would take me about five minutes. And
I arrived here late last Thursday night. It's now next
Sunday. So I've had plenty of time.

So have I told him?

Well, I've not yet managed to find those five minutes.

We've spent the week being cosy. Not snogging,
let alone anything more than snogging. Just a nice,
comfortable week together. We've not said anything
at all, we're just being good friends. To be honest,
I'm enjoying it – like Marlon and Tricia are, you
know, finding out about each other. I don't think I'm
being dishonest. Neil's not pushing, he's not taking
anything for granted, and there's no pressure. I'm
trying very hard not to lead him on, or lie to him, or
anything like that.

I'm not sure what's going through his head. With
blokes – with people – even if they're trying to keep
away from a tricky subject and they are trying to
keep their mouth shut, it's pretty easy to tell that it's
on their mind.

Paddy's like that – I can read him like a book. He
can't keep a secret from me, he's rubbish at it. I
thought he was the same with me: loads of times
where I've said 'Guess what I'm thinking?', Paddy
will tell me, word for word, with not a detail missing.
Recently, thankfully, he seems to have lost that
particular power – I really don't think he's got a clue
about Neil.

It's why I've been careful never to mention Neil.

Paddy doesn't know Dad's got a carer, let alone that it's a bloke, or he's called Neil. Because I know that if I ever said 'Neil', Paddy would hear the way I'd say it, and he'd instantly translate my tone of voice into what it really means 'Neil, this guy I fancy'.

I've never lied to Paddy. That is to say I've never told him anything untrue about Neil. He just doesn't know about him at all.

Paddy doesn't need to know, especially not now. Neil will be gone, Paddy will be there. I barely know Neil, and I guess in a couple of months I may even have begun to forget about him.

I've done that before. I saw an old school photo – back from when I was thirteen, something like that. And I really fancied this bloke. He was on the football team, and I think we snogged round the back of the youth centre once. My point is that at the time he was my world, I thought he was fantastic. If we did kiss, it was probably the highlight of my year, I must have thought about it every day.

But I can't even remember the boy's name now. He was either Larry or Loz, I think. And looking at the photo, there's just this greasy thirteen-year-old in a Batman T-shirt and a really bad mullet.

In a year's time, perhaps I won't even remember who Neil was. I won't have any photos of him, Dad won't mention him (he barely acknowledges Neil as it is). And that's a shame. Neil's a good bloke. We could have been good friends. What might have been. And it's not his fault at all.

With Dad more cheerful, and Neil being a great mate – and with the weather being surprisingly good at the moment – Southampton is so much more pleasant than it's ever been before.

I've not changed my mind.

I think I'm liking it here because I know it's coming to an end, the weight's been lifted.

That hasn't made it any easier to tell Neil what I've decided.

Today was the day Paddy was meant to be coming down here. Obviously that was out of the question. I phoned Paddy to tell him to hold his horses. Jason answered, and told me Paddy was busy packing the car. Paddy came to the phone, and I lied through my teeth.

'Dad's being a pain,' I told him. 'I need more time to talk him round.'

'Well, when should I come down? Tomorrow?'

'No!' I said quickly. 'I'll phone to tell you.'

'I'm all geared up, now,' Paddy said.

'You'll have to wait,' I told him. 'Only for a day or two, OK?'

Paddy obviously wasn't happy, but he agreed.

So that's bought me some more time.

But this can't go on. I need to tell Neil. I've worked myself up, I'm ready and raring to tell Neil what the score is. And after that, I can tell Dad about my plan.

But it's the evening, now, and Neil's gone home.

Tomorrow's the big day.

Monday 25 September

I'm cheating. This isn't really Monday, like it says there – I'm writing this on Tuesday morning.

Normally, when I get round to writing my diary, I do it last thing at night. There have been excep-tions – sometimes I do it during the day when I've had a spare moment or two, on a coach or waiting for Paddy to regain consciousness. Or I miss out days because I'm just too lazy, or I can't think of anything interesting that's happened. Usually, though, at least when I'm down in Southampton, I write up the day's events in bed, last thing before I go to sleep.

I couldn't write my diary last night because I was busy.

Guess what I was doing.

I told Neil.

I told him that Dad was moving up to Emmerdale. I explained that I was sure it was best for Dad – our house is just more sanitary than the place in Southampton, and there were plenty of Dingles in Emmerdale. He'd benefit from the country air, the pace of life would be more suited to a man of his age and health.

I also told Neil that the reason I'd come to the deci-sion I had was nothing whatsoever to do with my dad, or his health.

I told Neil I'd chosen to stay with Paddy, now and forever. That I did want to spend the rest of my life

with Paddy. That we were soul mates, that whatever
– whoever – else I met, no one could be better than
him. That, yes, if Paddy really wanted to, we'd be
starting a family. I want to grow old with him, I want
to spend the rest of my life in that small village in the
Yorkshire Dales, because I love Paddy more than
anything. Paddy's perfect, and I wouldn't change a
single thing, and I love him more than I've loved
anyone.

I told Neil that I liked him, and if Paddy wasn't
around, then I'd have jumped at the chance to be
with him. But I'd made up my mind.

Neil took it well.

He was upset, of course he was upset. I was upset
by that point. But he already knew that this was my
choice, and he knew me well enough to tell that I'd
made my choice, and he wasn't going to talk me out
of it. He didn't say anything, but I knew . . . he saw
how difficult the choice was, but that the choice had
been made. He could have made it so easy, he could
have ranted and raved, and made me glad to think
I was never going to see him again. Whatever he
said wouldn't make a difference – so he said nothing
at all.

And that almost made me change my mind.

'When?' he asked, after a minute.

'Tomorrow.'

That was the thing that shocked him.

'So soon?'

I nodded. 'It's best that way,' I told him.

He thought about that for a minute. 'You're right,' he said.

I'd wondered what he'd say when I told him. I guessed right – he'd accept my decision, hide his disappointment.

And he went off somewhere (to cry? I really don't know – I almost did).

I went into the front room, and told Dad that I couldn't keep coming down to Southampton, but I had a solution – he could come and live with us.

Dad glared at me for a minute – how dare his daughter dictate terms like that, and in his own house? – and then smiled.

'That could work,' he said very warily. 'Would that pig doctor husband of yours approve?'

'It were Paddy's idea.'

I'd said the wrong thing. Dad was suddenly suspicious. 'What's in it for him?'

'Nothing.'

'There's always something. No one does anything unless there's something in it for them.'

I didn't want to argue that point (not yet again, anyway).

'He doesn't think it's right that I spend so much time away from him and the life I've got in Emmerdale.'

Dad rubbed his chin. 'He may have a point.'

Something was the matter. I asked Dad what it was.

'That husband of yours is up to something, I'm sure of it. It's kind of you to offer, but no, no, I can't.'

I tried to think what on earth Paddy would ever want of Dad's. Everything my dad has is either thirty years old, broken or thirty years old and broken. I also tried to think of a way of telling my dad that in as tactful a way as possible. I needed to choose the right words and try not to wound his pride or make him feel like it had all been decided for him behind his back. Tact was needed. Tact and diplomacy.

The best I managed was to tell him he was talking a load of old rubbish, and that he shouldn't look a gift horse in the mouth – he was going to live rent and expenses-free in one of the most beautiful parts of the country. He could take it or leave it, but there was no doubt whatsoever that he if he said 'yes' he was going to be up on the deal and if he was too idiotic to see that then he could stuff the offer.

Dad looked a bit taken aback.

Then he thought about it.

'OK,' he said.

That afternoon Neil helped me to fill out the forms saying that Dad was moving, so we didn't need him to be a carer any more. Neil had popped out at lunchtime to pick them up. It felt like filling in a death warrant.

I asked him whether he was out of a job.

'No, I get tomorrow off, then on Monday I'll be over on Warren Avenue, looking after a woman called Denise who's in a wheelchair.'

'A young woman?' I asked.

'I'm not looking for romance at the moment,' he

told me. 'And we're not allowed to have "relation-
ships" with the people we're caring for. Not that the
subject ever came up with Caleb.'

We both laughed.

'So this is our last day together?' he asked.

'Yes,' I told him, the reality of that only just catching up with me. Tomorrow night . . . tonight at time of
writing, I'll be back in Emmerdale. Neil will be in the
past, I'd never see him again.

I didn't feel sad. It felt like the right thing to do.

I'll tell you what it felt like – it was like I'd come to
a fork in the road, and I'd already decided to go
right, but I could still see the other path.

I can do one thing or the other. I've chosen Paddy.

'Let's go out,' he said. 'Let's make it a night to
remember. A decent restaurant, then a couple of
decent bars and a decent club.'

I thought about that. I'd expected a quiet night in,
packing a suitcase, and trying to persuade Dad
which of his things he needed straight away, and
which could wait for a week or two. Neil's plan was
better. I knew what he was really saying – this is
going to end, so let's end on a high note. Let's enjoy
ourselves. Let's see what might have been.

I phoned Paddy first.

I phoned him just in case he phoned Dad tonight,
and Dad managed to tell Paddy all about Neil. That
would be typical, wouldn't it? Falling at the final
hurdle like that. One more night, and I've got away
with this.

I told Paddy that Dad needed just a <u>tad</u> more time to make up his mind. Paddy was disappointed that I couldn't tell him exactly when I wanted him to come down. (I don't want to say 'tomorrow' just in case Dad throws another wobbly).

But Paddy went away, and the rest of the night belonged to Neil.

I told Dad I wanted to thank Neil for all his hard work, so we were going out for a meal. I'd expected Dad to put his foot down, to insist I stayed with him. Instead he said: 'You don't need to do that, Mandy, Neil's just doing his job, you're not going to take the milkman out as well, are you? Or the bin men?'

This is the level of gratitude I can expect. It'll be nice having Dad living with us . . . but it's not going to be easy.

And, finally, after months, I got to go out.

Southampton by night – well, this time of year it's getting dark early again.

But the summer season's not quite over yet, there were all sorts of events. Somewhere (the Marina, Neil reckoned) there was a fireworks display.

First of all we went to a proper restaurant, not just a fish and chip place. The meal was wonderful stuff. Steak and potatoes, wine and strawberry ice cream. Neil didn't let me see the bill. It was a lot of money, though, that much was obvious. He's going to be eating nothing but baked beans for a couple of weeks to balance his books.

We went for a drink after that. I asked Neil if it was

his local, but he'd never been to the place before. I asked him if he'd be all right. He didn't want to answer at first, but finally he told me he would.

'A few weeks ago I didn't even know you,' he said. 'I'm glad I met you, you've made me happy again, reminded me my life isn't over. I'm sorry you're going, of course I am, but . . . well, life goes on.'

Once we felt up to it (we'd just eaten a huge meal, don't forget), we went to a club. It's a long time since Neil's been out dancing, but he soon got into the swing of it. We had a bit too much to drink, we cuddled and smooched on the dance floor.

And then we went back to his place. My first time there. It was smarter than I was expecting. A flat, but quite a big one. It was very modern – the sort of thing you see in magazines. I suppose when he split up he sold his house. Prices down here – well, he must have made a mint. So he spent money on doing up his new bachelor pad.

There aren't that many bachelor pads in Emmerdale. The only thing that comes close are all those lads living in Annie's Cottage. To give you some idea what that's like, the nearest thing they've got to an objet d'art is a neat pile of lager cans on the Welsh dresser. Neil's place couldn't have been more different. It was neat. All the washing-up was done, the magazines were all neatly tucked away in a magazine rack.

He apologized for the mess. The only thing I can think is that, knowing I was a Dingle, he must have thought I must find it difficult to make myself at home without half a broken washing machine in the room, or sitting on a sofa where the covering fit and all the springs still worked.

'Who decorated this place?' I said.

'I did.'

'You put that wooden floor down?'

He nodded. 'It's not that difficult.'

'Paddy can't even manage to put flat pack stuff together,' I told him.

His mouth moved, twitched. Was he about to say something, or make a joke, or was it just the lip quivering because he was upset, or tell me that I should leave him for someone with DIY skills? I don't know.

We sat next to each other on the armchairs. Gradually I drifted over, ending up sitting in front of him, with him brushing my hair. We talked, about <u>everything</u>. The details weren't important.

I told him that Paddy would never know about him. I would never even mention Neil's name to my husband.

'You're going to forget this ever happened?' Neil said.

'I won't,' I told him.

Silence. Comfortable silence.

'I keep a diary,' I told him. 'I started it just before I came down here.' And I explained why I'd decided to keep one.

'And you've written it all down? How there's this

idiot who's fallen for you, and how you're going back to your husband?'

'No one who falls for me could possibly be a complete idiot,' I laughed. 'I've written about the choice. And some days I would have chosen you. It's down there in black and white.'

'I was a close second?' he said, a bit surprised.

'Oh yes.'

I sat up and turned round, looked into his eyes. 'And now it's goodbye.'

Neil sighed. 'I've never been very good at saying goodbye. I never really know—'

I kissed him. And it became more than a kiss, and he joined me down on the floor, and this time I knew exactly what I was doing, I wasn't getting carried away. I wasn't surprised it had happened this time.

'You understand?' I asked him.

'I do. This is only for tonight. It's your way of saying goodbye.'

'I don't want to forget you. You'll always be special.'

And then he took my hand and led me to the bedroom and . . . well, use your imagination.

I was the second woman he'd ever slept with. I didn't know that until afterwards. His wife and me. If I'd have known, then I probably would have had second thoughts about doing it. It means a lot to me that we did what we did – but it's going to mean more to Neil, I think.

I didn't plan it. Even up to the moment I kissed

him, I wasn't planning it. I know no one would believe that – I can almost hear them: 'Come off it, Mand. A romantic meal, drinks, dancing and back to his place . . . what did you think would happen?' Well, I wasn't thinking that far ahead.

I think the fact it wasn't planned helped – neither of us had time to get nervous, or to let any proprieties or anxiety get in the way. Can I explain why it happened in words? No – but it feels right that it happened. Like when I undressed him – no surprises, no tattoos, or scars, or a six-pack or anything, just what I was expecting. But neither of us suddenly got shy, or had second thoughts. You know if it feels right, and it did.

So, was it the greatest night of my life? No – there was absolutely nothing wrong with it, and we both enjoyed ourselves, but it felt, I don't know, <u>friendly</u>, rather than raw passion. Like it was unfinished business, rather than the culmination of some great romance. Between times (yes <u>times</u> – look, I'm not going into details, OK?!), we talked, and dozed off, and just held each other.

When I compare Neil with Paddy . . . and comparisons are inevitable, aren't they? Neil was a bit of a disappointment. Paddy knows me better, knows what I like, and we're used to each other. But even the first time, even with Paddy's lack of experience, it was better. We knew we were soulmates, the connection was a lot more than physical. With Neil, I got the feeling he was doing what he used to do with his wife, when she let him. I don't know what I was expecting, but it was a bit routine. I had a good time, don't get me wrong, but I've had better. Probably just as well. If he'd pulled off his shirt and looked like Russell Crowe and then shown me what I've been missing, then perhaps I'd have second thoughts about going back to Paddy.

I woke up next to Neil this morning, and it didn't feel strange at all. Last night it crossed my mind, briefly, that this was going to be the awkward bit – the bit where the rules of etiquette break down a bit. Was I meant to slip out of bed and go home in the middle of the night, or be up and dressed by the time he woke up? But in the end, we both woke up about the same time – no idea what that time is: later than I think it is, probably. He brought me breakfast in bed, then got back in, and we talked, among other things. And being in bed without a nightie but with a man who isn't my husband didn't feel wrong at all.

He's in the shower now, and there's an unspoken agreement, I think, that the next time we see each other, we'll be dressed and we won't be discussing last night again.

Well. I've got a few more minutes lying in Neil's bed, letting my memories catch up with me. It's a good mattress, and the sheets are lovely and soft against the skin – I wonder if it's the done thing to ask what fabric softener he uses? Or would using it just remind me of Neil every time I woke up next to Paddy?

I feel good. This is the first day of the rest of my life.

Thinking back, I feel a bit guilty. I slept with another man. Do you know – the whole of last night, I didn't think about Paddy once? I've spent so long weighing things up between Paddy and Neil. I've had a choice, haven't I? But when that bedroom door shut, there was only Neil, and it was like Paddy didn't exist. That sounds so wrong, doesn't it? There was no guilt last night, just calmness. If I had my time over, I'd do exactly the same thing again – Paddy will never know, I've satisfied my curiosity, Neil got at least one thing he was after, Paddy's got nothing to worry about, and now I know, once and for all, that I want to be with him for the rest of my life. No one gets hurt.

So what would I think of Paddy if I found out he'd done what I did last night?

I . . . suspected him of it once. Jane, that old school friend who worked in a bank, and who his mum wanted him to marry. She always dressed like she was going to an interview, not a hair out of place, lipstick perfect. She really liked Paddy and she didn't have a boyfriend. But Paddy never did anything. I know that. Even when we split up, he didn't go after Jane, or show any interest in anyone else. He went to the Vets' Ball with Bernice, but that was because you've got to have a woman on your arm at a do like that. He's been out socially with other women, but would never even think about it.

He's not the type. I'm Paddy's first and only. I don't think he's ever been curious about anyone else.

I'm not the type, either. Or at least I'm not any more – before I met Paddy I wasn't quite as restrained. I wasn't a wild child, anything like that, but I had a normal, healthy love-life. But adultery's a new one on me. Never done that before.

It feels good now it's out of the way. Like there's a chapter of my life closing, a little story with a beginning, a middle and now an end. If I hadn't slept with Neil, I think it would have always nagged at me – what sort of lover would he have been, would I have been happier? All those sort of questions.

This is exactly what I wanted. I wanted to have my cake and eat it. And I've had that, now, so I can get on, get back to Paddy and Emmerdale and get on with my life, putting this part of my life behind me.

Wednesday 27 September

No.

No. ~~Paddy was there when I got~~.

~~I woke up this morning thinking~~

~~It could have~~

Paddy came down to Southampton. He didn't phone first, I wasn't expecting him.

I went back to Dad's house with Neil. At about seven. Seven in the evening.

I said I didn't know what time it was yesterday when I was writing my diary. It turned out it was eleven in the morning. I also said something about an unspoken agreement about being dressed and businesslike next time we saw each other.

We reneged on that deal.

Neil came back in as I was gathering my clothes off the floor. He was dressed, and I wasn't and . . . well, we didn't even get as far as the bed. Then I had a shower, then Neil helped me scrub my back, and then we <u>did</u> get as far as the bed.

By the time we were both dressed, it was starting to get dark, and we had this horrible *Home Alone* moment as we realized we'd left Dad by himself all day.

So we hurried back home.

We were being playful, enjoying ourselves. It was like the last day of term at school – we'd had a good time, but it was over. Demob happy, I think it's called. We both knew where we stood, and we were still feeling pleased with ourselves because of what we'd been doing all day. This wasn't going to be a tearful farewell – we both thought it was great that someone found us sexy, and that we were being so grown up about it.

I told Neil straight – I loved Paddy, and nothing he could say would possibly make me change my mind. Neil accepted my decision, but teased me all the way home.

'Where are you going to tell your dad you were last night?'

'I'm a big girl, now.'

'Am I a big boy?'

That sort of thing.

Harmless banter.

But Neil was already history.

I wanted him to go, to be honest – the line was drawn. My job now was to get Dad ready to move, then get on with the rest of my life. I didn't think he'd come back with me – he was just being polite, he said. It felt a bit like being followed around by a puppy that you wish would have just stayed where it was.

But Neil was so sweet, we'd had such a great night together (and I don't just mean once we got to his bedroom), that I couldn't really resent him. So I was happy to hold hands and cuddle up and act like a young couple very much in love. We <u>were</u> a young couple in love. I love Neil. Loved him. We knew it was coming to an end, but we didn't want it to.

And we were being so pleased with ourselves, that I didn't even notice Paddy's car outside Dad's house. How could I have missed it? It's this great big 4x4 thing. And it was right there in front of the house.

I can't remember the exact words Neil and I were saying, not all of them. It wouldn't have mattered, not normally. It was just banter. I was saying that Neil shouldn't come in. It was already over between us. We were saying goodbye, forever, but because of what we said . . .

I was in the hall, Neil hovered on the doorstep.

I didn't want a scene. Not right at the last minute, just as everything was falling into place. It had been so perfect. If Neil went now, without any fuss, then I'd have everything I wanted. Neat and tidy, no fallout. I felt guilty for betraying Paddy, but he would never know, and there was no chance at all I would ever go back to Neil. What I've learnt, what I've come to realize over the last couple of months, is that I love Paddy more than anyone. That I want to spend the rest of my life with him. If he wants babies . . . well, I don't, not yet, but he may even be able to talk me round on that one. If my dad's not got long (and he hasn't), then it's selfish of me to wait much longer. My dad would love me to give him a grandson. And hear his first words, watch his first steps. We've discussed it – there was no pressure from Dad, it was just a general discussion about how much he likes seeing Key around the place.

But all of that was the future, and Neil has nothing to do with my future, and I wanted to gently push him away now, so I could get on with the rest of my life, like we'd agreed.

Then Neil said that I shouldn't phone Paddy just yet – he thought we should have one more night together like last night. Neil was being much too serious when he suggested that, I thought. When I didn't reply he blurted out, 'Don't go.'

I said, as calmly as I could, 'Neil, please don't do this to me.'

'Mandy, please,' he begged. 'All I'm asking is for

you to give us a chance. You know it could work.'

He was so upset I couldn't stop the tears, even when I said as firmly as I could, 'There is no *us*, Neil. There never can be. I'm married.'

'Then what was last night all about? And today? You weren't thinking about him then, were you? All this time we've had—'

'Last night, dinner and . . . everything . . . it was just supposed to be goodbye . . .'

'All our time together, it must have meant something to you.'

'Oh, it has. I should have stopped coming here the moment I realized but I couldn't. I just had to be with you,' I said. I wanted him to know at least that my feelings were real.

'Then stay with me. I could make you happy,' he pleaded.

'I can't. I love Paddy. He needs me,' I said.

'I need you,' Neil cried.

It was too much. All I could say, through the tears was, 'Oh Neil, I'm so sorry. I'm so sorry.'

And then Paddy walked out of the front room, into the hall.

And my world collapsed.

It all went wrong in that one moment. Conjunctions. Like I said before. If one thing had been slightly different. If Neil hadn't followed me back, if we'd seen Paddy's car, or spotted Paddy in the lounge through the window. If Paddy had turned up five minutes later, or if he'd just heard what we'd been saying just a moment before, when I said I loved Paddy.

I just wish Paddy knew what I'd been <u>thinking</u>, instead of hearing me admit I had wanted to be with another man. Why was I trying so hard not to hurt Neil's feelings? Someone I was never going to see again. Looking back on it, I can hardly bear to imagine what Paddy was thinking.

Did he even know Neil existed? Only if my dad mentioned him. How long had he been waiting in my dad's front room?

'What are you doing here?' I asked.

I knew exactly what he was doing here. Catching me red-handed.

Paddy's face . . . he's usually so mild a person, he hides his emotions a lot of the time, keeps it bottled up. I've never seen anyone so upset. Or anyone so angry. Or humiliated. Or embarrassed. Or hateful, or . . . He didn't even look at me – he looked straight at me, and straight through me. His world had just gone. Everything about his world had gone, and you could see it in his eyes.

Could he see that on my face, too? What expression did I have on my face? Did he just see a liar, a cheat, an unfaithful wife? He wouldn't have known, would he? He thought he knew me, that he could read me like a book. But he couldn't have had any warning of this. Even if Dad or Adam or his own instincts were telling him there was something odd going on, then he'd have discounted their advice. He knew me, and this just wasn't something I did.

In a second . . . in less than a second, he realized that he didn't know what I was thinking, that what he thought and the reality of the situation were so far apart that he had nothing he could take for granted.

I know that I was horrified, destroyed, by that moment. I saw Paddy's face and knew that's just how I was feeling: ashamed with myself, unable to believe I had done something so wrong and unlike me. But Paddy could be forgiven for thinking it was just the shock of a woman being caught doing something wrong.

If he thinks that, he's dead wrong. A few weeks ago, yes, but . . .

I love him. I know that. And that look on his face. I know I love him now, I'm certain of it.

But he doesn't love me now. I saw his face and . . . all trace of that had gone.

Adam was there. What was Adam doing there? He gave me this look – a real 'I knew all along' look. That time he caught me phoning Neil. He must have realized what was going on – perhaps he'd overheard more than I thought he had.

But Paddy was already out the door, Adam trailing after him.

I need to get back to Emmerdale. There's one more coach tonight and I'll be on it. I'm starting to hate that journey but at least I'll get some time to figure out exactly what I am going to say to Paddy.

I couldn't stay in the house with Dad, I couldn't be with Neil. I went for a walk on the Common. You can imagine what I was thinking, I don't need to spell it out.

I have to get Paddy back.

But I already know it's too late. Deep down, I know he won't have me back. And I don't blame him at all.

Thursday 28 September

I've left.

Not just Paddy, but also the Dingles and Emmerdale.

I have to write more than that, I know. But really, it doesn't matter what was said, now.

The only thing that matters is that it's all over, and I've left Emmerdale forever, and it's like it's all over, end of story, end of Mandy.

I arrived in Emmerdale last night and went straight to Paddy and we talked for a whole night and day, without stopping to eat or sleep. Just the two of us, going over everything. At some points both of us were trying to find a way out of it, at others we were justifying why it was all over. Broken crockery one moment, hugs and kisses the next. Could it have turned out differently? For all the ground we covered, for all the things we said, I really think this was the only way it could have ended. But we had to try, and we both so wanted it to work out differently. We both wanted it to be the way it had been. But you can never go home again. Things had changed, forever.

I'm exhausted now. Not just physically tired, although I certainly am that – they had to wake me up at Southampton. I've said everything I can possibly have said on the subject. My emotions . . . I'm not going to cry or laugh or get angry for a while, I just can't, I've used up all my reserves of that. I feel dead inside, like I've ceased to exist.

I can't give you a blow by blow account of the whole conversation, just what I remember. And none of it is important, not now; it's all history.

Paddy wanted to know what he'd done wrong. I told him the honest answer – nothing. I told him about Neil, I told him about Neil and how it had just happened.

When I said that, it brought home just how wrong the things I had done were. How many lies there had been – not just the obvious ones, like not mentioning Neil, or the fact that all the time I'd been in Emmerdale this summer I'd been thinking about another man. There were other secrets, there was hypocrisy – the fact that I could stand up in the middle of the Woolpack and tell everyone that Kelly was terrible for having an affair, when I was doing just the same. The fact that I knew about Kelly and Scott sleeping together, and never told Paddy, who worked with Kelly and had to deal with the aftermath of her suicide attempt. I never even hinted that I knew.

Paddy slagged off the Dingles. We go on about family loyalty, and when someone causes us a prob-

lem, like Tara wanting to evict us, or the Tates killing
Butch, we rally round. But the rest of the time . . . he
reminded me about Nellie, Zak's first wife. When she
showed up earlier in the year, she quickly wormed
her way back into Zak's bed. I had forgotten all
about that, but it was exactly the same thing I'd done
with Neil. Lisa was completely innocent, but Zak was
weak. Only once, as he tells it, but there's no such
thing as 'only once' in situations like this.

The Dingles by marriage are always expected to
live up to the Dingle Code, to be part of the family.
And they all do it: Lisa, Emily, even Paddy – they
accept the rules, they become part of the family and
they behave honourably and loyally. Emily married
a Dingle on his deathbed and she's going to spend
the rest of her life faithful to a man she hardly even
touched. She'll die a virgin because of her loyalty
and honesty.

But the Dingles themselves, those of us that are
born Dingles, we cheat, lie and conveniently forget
the rules when it suits us.

Paddy's right: Lisa did nothing wrong, Paddy did
nothing wrong. The whole Dingle Law . . . we always
go on about other people: the law, the council, the
rich, the landowners, the snobs. But really the
Dingles have always been our own worst enemy. It's
us – our greed, our stupidity, our belief that the world
owes us a living and nothing bad we ever do can
ever have consequences or hurt anyone.

And without patronizing me, or pitying me, or

looking down or anything like that, Paddy just spelt it out to me – he had played it by the Dingle Code, he'd done everything right, he'd cut his ties with his own mother to be with me. In return, I'd cheated on him, broken the Dingle Code, done something that was unforgivable.

Paddy told me that when he was recovering from his accident he realized how precious life was, how much he valued what he had. And he thought that the best thing about his life was me. That I was the best thing that had ever happened to him.

I told him that I'd realized that, too. I agreed with him. I didn't want to leave.

I told him that we'd both known we'd had a problem. Nothing big, nothing particularly unusual – just that phase every relationship goes through, if it lasts long enough, where things have settled down, but some things have settled in slightly the wrong place. We'd both sensed it, we'd both questioned ourselves about it and thought it through. We hadn't been able to talk because I'd either been on the other side of the country, and it wasn't the sort of thing you could do on the phone, or I'd been in Emmerdale but we'd never quite got round to talking about it.

And being with Neil had been fun, it had shown me what I was missing. I loved Neil. But what it had done is made me realize just how much I had with Paddy, compared with just fun, or just that thrill of the chase, or of having someone lusting after me. I had that as well with Paddy, but I'd lost sight of it. I told Paddy if he could forgive me then I would come back and love him more than ever.

I didn't have any excuses, I told him.

It's true. I can't explain why I fell for Neil, or come up with a neat list of reasons I did what I did. I know it wasn't because Paddy had done something wrong, or he was inadequate in any way ... it wasn't his fault. So how could he ever do anything to stop me from straying again? How could he be sure that I wouldn't?

I can't answer that one. All I could do is say that I'd ask myself the same question.

Everything I said sounded so hollow. I'd only done it once, I only did it because we were splitting up, Paddy wasn't supposed to know, I'd already decided that I loved Paddy and wanted to spend the rest of my life with him.

I wouldn't have believed me.

But Paddy believed me. He didn't argue about that. I'd have screamed blue murder, 'Only once?!' and stuff like that. I told Paddy I wished I was dead, and I did, I really wished the ground would open up and swallow me. I told him I would go, and that I was going upstairs to pack some things. Paddy clung on to me, told me not to be so stupid. We held each other, cried, and then ... then we were tearing each others' clothes off, and doing it there and then, and for two or three minutes all our problems went away, and there was more passion, more emotion, than any number of Neils. We held each other close, sobbing and laughing and just didn't talk, or think, or remember, or care. And everything was going to be all right.

As we tucked ourselves back in, Paddy showed me the eternity ring he'd bought for our anniversary. It was beautiful ... but the anniversary is in October, and we both knew that we weren't going to get that far.

Paddy said that no one is perfect. He made the mistake of thinking I was perfect. And that illusion's broken, now. He's realized just how often I must have lied to him. I told you Paddy was clever, I told you that he knew me. He's just thought back, and worked out exactly what had been going on. He can't believe he didn't spot it. But the reason he didn't was that he wasn't looking. I didn't think I would, he just didn't think it was possible.

He couldn't have loved me more. He loved me as I was, or as he thought I was – he didn't want me back humbled, and sorry for what I'd done, knowing he could never trust me again, always looking for signs of infidelities and that I was keeping secrets from him.

He told me about the night he'd proposed, when he realized I'd followed him to the Vets' Ball but fled without him seeing me. He'd come back to the village, knowing I'd been there, and he'd found me crying in Pollard's barn.

That night, he said, he'd heard music. We both

had. None had been playing, but we heard it anyway, and we danced and he proposed.

But now the music had stopped. The song was over.

And we both knew he was right. He thought we could give it another go. He thought there was a chance. But he was wrong. It was over. I left the ring on the table and walked out of Emmerdale.

I was exhausted. I don't even remember getting to Hotten or buying a ticket or boarding the coach. I slept all the way to Southampton.

And now Southampton's home.

Friday 29 September

So now what?

Today is the first day of the rest of my life.

Ha!

I'm lying in a council house in Southampton on a mattress which was stolen from a prison in a tiny, poky bedroom. My mattress, my bedroom. It's my home, now.

I don't want to get up, I don't want to face the morning, or my dad's questions. I'll have to, and I'm sure he'll understand. He's delighted to have me back. He knows I've had an argument with Paddy, but he doesn't realize I won't be going back to him. How will he react? He'll be glad to have his daughter back, I think. That's a question for another day. I don't want to go through it with Dad just yet. I've said everything I could say to Paddy, I wrote it all down in my diary. I just feel numb, now, I don't want to go through all that again, not yet.

There's no chance of me going back. Paddy deserves better. I can't live with Zak, with his stupid Dingle Code that none of our stupid family follow unless it suits us or there's something in it for us.

I can't even think about who's going to care for my dad.

Me, of course. But will social services really be able to find another carer? One thing I do I know for sure is that Neil's not coming back – he's been reassigned, remember? We filled in all those forms together, and he'll be looking after Denise, now, the woman with a wheelchair.

I love Paddy. I'm married. It's coming up to our wedding anniversary. 13 October. We didn't even make it to our first anniversary. Even Michael Jackson and Lisa Marie made it to their first anniversary. Patsy and Liam lasted more than a year. My marriage to Butch lasted almost as long as this.

I know now that I'll never be able to go back to Emmerdale. That's it. Out.

I was wrong.

There's just no question of that. Paddy did nothing wrong whatsoever. I felt that some of the spice and spontaneity had gone . . . well, it was always going to, wasn't it, if I went racing off to look after my dad rather than spending time with my husband?

But even then that makes it sounds like it's my dad's fault for being ill.

And it was my fault.

Mine alone.

So what does that mean? That I go round to Neil's house and say Paddy didn't work out and so the runner-up gets the prize after all? The morning after we slept together, I told Neil I don't love him as much as Paddy. And I don't. He knows that, I know that. He said in that letter that he likes the fact I get what I want, I've been saying all along that I don't want to <u>settle</u> for second-best, I want it all.

And, though I love him, Neil's second best. And I'd rather have nothing than that.

Could I grow to love him as much? Well, read this diary back for the answer to that one. I loved Neil, I loved what he <u>meant</u> – but I was with Paddy out of choice, not because no one else would have me. If I wanted to, I could have left Paddy.

But I don't want to leave Paddy.

Didn't want to leave. I have left him.

I love him. He's my husband, we've been through so much.

So why aren't I up in Emmerdale now, camped outside the cottage shouting up to Paddy, telling him I love him, and can never leave him?

Because I don't have a leg to stand on.

Paddy's right not to forgive me.

It's not that I've broken the Dingle Code, or anything like that. It's far more basic. I've lied to him, for such a long time. And I did it so easily, he didn't even notice. If I could do that now, then I could do it at any point in the future. How could he ever trust me again?

And what did I lie for? For the good of my family or because I had a great and secret love for someone? No, I did it for a boring bloke who I had a crush on. I kept that quiet, I jumped into bed with him after one meal, a couple of drinks and him brushing my hair. The fact is that if I could lie and cheat to keep Neil a secret, then there must be a million other blokes out there that I'd do exactly the same for.

Paddy stayed loyal. If he'd done what I'd done, I wouldn't just tell him to get lost, I'd do a little impromptu bobbitting on him with a kitchen knife.

I've thrown away marriage with the man I love for . . . nothing. Nothing at all. There is no way at all in which I've gained.

I've lost so much.

I did my horoscope.

It didn't help at all, it was all in the past tense. I've burned my bridges, I've had a disaster in love, there is a great distance now between my friends and home. I know all that – I'm looking for the answer, the way out. But it's over. It's like I ceased to exist the moment I left Paddy and the village.

What's the use of a prediction if it only tells what's already happened, not what's happening next week?

I've been flicking through my diary.

I can see where I went wrong, I'm reading it now going 'No, don't do that!'. There are so many ways I could have avoided this situation, and so many times it almost happened before it did. I was worried about what people thought about me, I was worried that if you just judged me by appearances you'd think I was just a bundle of fun with a loud mouth and louder blouses. That if people knew what I was thinking, then they'd think differently – see there was more to me than met the eye, that I had thoughts and secrets that you wouldn't begin to suspect.

I only wish I'd been wrong.